Praise for the Rosalind Mystery series

THE FUNDY VAULT

"*The Fundy Vault* is a page-turner with gravitas.... Corporate thugs, implicated local authorities, and a theatre cast's foreboding lines from Samuel Beckett conspire to pull us into an undertow of suspense."

—PATRICIA REIS, author of *Motherlines* and *Women's Voices*

"An excellent follow-up to *Foul Deeds*, this is more than just a mystery: it's a love story to the Bay of Fundy and to the art of making theatre. A very timely crime brings back the characters I loved in the first Rosalind Mystery.... Couldn't put it down. This is a cracking summer read!"

—DAVID MCCLELLAND, actor, filmmaker, director

"Linda Moore has rooted her story so deeply in this place you can almost feel the sand under your feet and the water dripping from its caves. Moore's characters are feisty, her plots intriguing, and she writes with a light, intelligent touch. I'm so happy to see this new Rosalind Mystery. May there be many more."

—WENDY LILL, Governor General's Award–nominated playwright

"From the breathtaking natural power of the Fundy coast to the uncanny beauty of a Beckett play, Linda Moore's latest Rosalind Mystery sweeps the reader along on a rising tide of suspense with a plot that is action-packed, timely, and full of dramatic tension."

—JANET MUNSIL, award-winning playwright

"Moore's deft plotting and flowing dialogue brings us a compelling story of modern greed in a timeless place. Nova Scotia's Bay of Fundy is a sweeping backdrop to a suspenseful, well-wrought story. Rosalind's oddball troupe of actors parses Samuel Beckett's short plays, and his dystopic view of the human condition has an eerie resonance with the cynical crime she witnesses. Compelling and well paced, Moore's second Rosalind Mystery transports us with insight, wit and engaging characters."

–MARY-COLIN CHISHOLM, award-winning actor, director, artistic co-director of LunaSea Theatre, and playwright

"Linda Moore, a Canadian original, has been creating dynamic narratives in the theatre for forty years. In *The Fundy Vault*, Ms. Moore spins the story with such intimacy and Beckettian craft, I felt as though I was sitting in her study being told the tale by candlelight, the Nova Scotian wind rattling the windowpanes."

–DEAN GABOURIE, artistic director

"The characters, as in *Foul Deeds*, continue their fascination and the plot keeps us totally on edge…a page turner."

–LEON MAJOR, first artistic director, Neptune Theatre

FOUL DEEDS

"Like Shakespeare, Linda Moore understands the human heart and the foul deeds to which our hearts can sometimes drive us. From beginning to end, this novel is riveting."

–GAIL BOWEN, author of the Joanne Kilbourn mysteries

THE FUNDY VAULT

A Rosalind Mystery

LINDA MOORE

Vagrant
PRESS

Nimbus Publishing Limited
3731 Mackintosh St, Halifax, NS B3K 5A5
(902) 455-4286 nimbus.ca

Printed and bound in Canada

NB1229

This novel is a work of fiction. Names, characters, places, and incidents are either the product of the author's imagination or are used fictitiously. Any resemblance to actual persons, living or dead, events or locales is entirely coincidental.

Library and Archives Canada Cataloguing in Publication

Moore, Linda, 1950-, author
The Fundy vault / Linda Moore.
(A Rosalind mystery) Sequel to: Foul deeds.
Issued in print and electronic formats.

ISBN 978-1-77108-421-5 (paperback). —ISBN 978-1-77108-422-2 (html)
I. Title. II. Series: Moore, Linda, 1950- . Rosalind mystery.

PS8626.O5945F86 2016   C813'.6   C2016-903746-0
                                      C2016-903747-9

Nimbus Publishing acknowledges the financial support for its publishing activities from the Government of Canada through the Canada Book Fund (CBF) and the Canada Council for the Arts, and from the Province of Nova Scotia. We are pleased to work in partnership with the Province of Nova Scotia to develop and promote our creative industries for the benefit of all Nova Scotians.

to the Bay of Fundy

Acknowledgements

Whitney Moran, senior editor of Nimbus, for thoughtful encouragement and oversight in bringing this project to completion

Kate Kennedy, editor, for tireless attention to detail and guidance

Sandra McIntryre, founder of Vagrant Press, who provided excellent editorial advice during the early days of this project

E. Alex Pierce for passionate, profound insight throughout

Jim Harrod for geological ruminations

Lulu Keating for generous feedback on every visit home, and the wise listeners:
Sandy Moore, Patricia Reis, Carolyn Hethrington, Paula Danckert, Mary-Ellen MacLean, Wendy Katherine, and Christina Wheelwright

The long-ago porch party on Longspell Road, where I read the first two chapters and this undertaking began in earnest

The late great Jest in Time Theatre Company, and our unforgettable expedition into the Beckett oeuvre

Chapter 1

If I had just kept my nose in my book—if only I hadn't looked up when I heard the crows...

~

I WAS RENTING A COTTAGE on the Minas Basin, along the coast that runs from Kingsport, Nova Scotia, up to Cape Blomidon. It would be a much-needed break from my job in Halifax, and a chance to recharge my batteries. It was 6 o'clock and the spring morning was surprisingly warm. I couldn't wait to get out there.

I shoved an orange and a couple of books into my old rucksack, stepped out, and crossed the grass to the edge of the bluff. To the east the sun was climbing over the basin. Below me, the tide was on its way out, revealing vast stretches of sand and clay.

I climbed down to the beach via several rickety apple ladders strung together from the clifftop to the rocky base. The gulls were scrapping over the tiny crabs, mussels, and other tasty bits being served up as the water's edge receded. A little further into the wash, the herons stood, silent and tall, perusing their spoils.

I picked my way through the rocks to the smooth red sand. To my right I could see the village pier about half a mile from where I stood. Just before the pier was a public beach where a couple of dogs were jouking about in the water. Otherwise, all was deserted.

Glorious solitude!

We were only a couple of days into June, yet the sun on my arms felt as warm as midsummer. I spread out a towel, sat, and leaned my back against a large rock, breathed deep, and felt the stress of a hectic winter drop away.

For once in my life I had a real job, and it included a real vacation. I was a trained criminologist. My proving ground had been the several years I'd spent freelancing with my irascible old pal, Private Investigator McBride. While often a choice of last resort, McBride had shown himself best in the business. Wily and intuitive, he could untangle the knots of a crime like no one else—and often managed to solve cases that had been long abandoned by the law.

But almost a year ago, I had begun working as a full-time researcher with the Public Prosecution Service. While I was eager to have the job, the rampant greed and corruption that characterized most crimes we prosecuted was overwhelming, and I was ready for a breather.

Despite my full-time job, I was determined to eke out a place for my other occupation—or obsession, perhaps—as a dramaturg, assisting theatre artists on plays they were producing. I had just begun an intriguing project with a small but mighty physical theatre company, putting together a presentation of short dramatic works by the Irish playwright Samuel Beckett. We were selecting the pieces we wanted to explore, and I had brought along several Beckett scripts and a variety of books about his life and writing. This luxurious vacation would give me time to zero in on the material without distractions.

I was digging through my rucksack for the script of his play *Catastrophe*, a brief but startling political metaphor, when a gang of nearby crows erupted in a rowdy fracas.

I looked up and over to my left. There they were! At least two dozen of them, their black wings shiny in the sun. They were gathered in the dense treetops over Longspell Point, which juts into the Minas Basin where the shoreline turns to the north.

No wonder they call them a murder of crows, I thought. That racket would do anybody in!

A sudden sharp breeze blew in from the northeast, strong enough to push along an enormous floating tree trunk with a craggy mass of black gnarled roots. Many of the branches were broken and dragging through the water, but some still reached up, leafing in vain. Several of the crows launched together, flew out over the water, and circled the broken tree as it rounded the point. It was moving rapidly from my far left into the middle of the basin in front of me. The details were too far away to discern, but there appeared to be some brightly coloured blue and red cloth snarled into the roots—a towel perhaps. I took off my sunglasses, leaned forward, and squinted, trying to see.

Then I stood, alarmed. I started running along the shore towards the village pier, hoping to find someone who might corroborate what I was seeing. Coming towards me was a woman walking the two dogs I had seen playing earlier, a little yappy dog and a very large dog.

"Hi," I said, stopping in front of her and catching my breath. "I'm Rosalind…I'm renting—"

"Lovely morning." She extended her hand. "Grace."

I shook it. "Can I ask you something?" I said.

"What is it?"

"Do you see that fallen tree way out there being blown towards the opposite shore?"

"Oh, yes, that's not an uncommon sight," she responded. "It's the erosion, especially in the spring—the trees crash down off the bluff onto the beach. Then they're tossed about by the wind and the tides, and pulled into open water."

"But is it just me, or can you make out something very strange there—wound into the roots. See the coloured cloth—the sheet or whatever...."

"How do you mean strange?" she asked.

"Like...a person?"

We were facing south and the sun was still climbing just to the east of where we were looking. She put her hand up to shade her eyes and moved towards the water's edge. The crows were still making a ruckus, circling the trunk, landing, flying. "I do see something tangled there, but a person? No, I'd say that's a little far-fetched. I'd say it's floating plastic and garbage that's gotten caught in the roots. There's more and more debris out there these days, unfortunately."

"But the crows...."

"Well, crows are scavengers—they love garbage, don't they? Nice to meet you, Rosalind. Enjoy your stay. On we go!"

"And carrion. They love carrion," I muttered, as she continued on towards the point, her two dogs frolicking ahead of her.

Was she right? Was I just imagining an actual person caught there? I looked out across the water once again. I tried not to see them, but I could still discern human arms tangled into the dark roots.

Pursuing this "far-fetched" notion was the last thing I wanted to do. I was here to escape, if only for a couple of weeks, from the grim realities of crime. That was my plan: nature's beauty, Beckett, and lots of sleep.

I threw my things into my rucksack and clambered back up the apple ladders. I stood in the glassed-in porch holding the shiny new BlackBerry I had purchased just before leaving Halifax. I wasn't sure where to start but I decided to call the nearest fire department.

The fellow who answered—Stan—asked if I was from the city, called me dear, and spoke at length about the tides. "Six hours and thirteen minutes out, six hours and thirteen minutes in," he said. As to what I thought I had seen, he shared Grace's skepticism. He suggested I alert the RCMP if I was really concerned.

∽

Within half an hour two young officers rolled up to my rented cottage. I watched them as they stood on the cliff's edge with their high-powered binoculars trying to determine whether this was a wild goose chase. A stronger wind was now blowing from the east and had pushed the floating mass of branches around so its roots faced the opposite shore. This made it almost impossible to see the lower section of the trunk from where we stood. Constable Brad Cudmore lowered his binoculars and looked around. "Pretty nice out here eh?"

I nodded.

He glanced over at his partner and then strolled off towards the cruiser. Clearly, he was done. His partner, Corporal Riley Monaghan, a sparky young woman no taller than five feet, was showing more determination. She moved a few steps along the cliff's edge and looked again, and then repeated the action.

"Come on!" she said, encouraging the tree. "Come on, turn a little bit more, just a little bit more…oh my sweet Jesus!" she suddenly blurted. "You're right—I think it is a person—a woman? Yup, you're right! I see her now—you can almost see her face. Take a look." She thrust her binoculars at me, as the startled Constable Cudmore lurched up from the rear fender and hustled back towards us. I lifted the binoculars.

Yes, there she was! The crystal clear image caught my breath. She had red hair and her skin was so pale as to be almost blue, her arms reaching into the dark roots. She looked like Ophelia in the pre-Raphaelite drowning paintings except her body was wound in what I now realized was neither a towel nor a sheet.

"Is that what I think it is?" I wondered aloud.

Corporal Riley Monaghan nodded. "Yes, Ma'am—you're not just whistling Dixie. That's an American flag."

Chapter 2

I HAD NO CHOICE. I had to call McBride.

"So, she's dead?" he asked.

"She looks dead," I replied. "The RCMP think so—they're arranging a Zodiac, or some kind of boat for high tide. When I told them I was a criminologist, they agreed to let me ride along. Why don't you drive out here, McBride? Come and take a look! Bring Molly—she'd love a run on the beach." Molly was McBride's black lab—and a bona fide member of the team, having saved us both from harm on more than one occasion.

"I don't know, Roz. Molly's depressed," McBride said. "Doesn't want to go out…she just lies on the hall carpet all day and sighs. She misses Sophie."

"Oh, I see, it's Molly's fault you haven't left your house in over a week. You're sure that's not you lying on the hall carpet moping about Sophie? Get off your duff, McBride. Come and do a little investigating."

Sophie was an old and dear theatre friend of mine, an actress, who had met McBride during a murder case he and I were working on. She had been abducted while getting information for us from an informer, and McBride had heroically rescued her. This precipitated a passionate romance between them, and on an impulse they decided to get married. Now time had passed, and Sophie was taking a little hiatus from the marriage. A few weeks prior, she had made an abrupt decision to go to Toronto to follow up on some audition possibilities and hadn't let McBride know when she'd be coming home. I'd been doing my best to keep my advice and opinions out of it—but I had seen the rocky road ahead, even before the wedding.

"Hang on," I said. I could hear the distinct rhythm of a helicopter. I looked out through the large porch windows. Flying low, it advanced across the Minas Basin and hovered over the broken tree trunk, which by now had been blown further towards the opposite shore and was partly bobbing in the surf and caught on an emerging sandbar.

"It looks like the Mounties aren't going to wait for the tide," I said. "They've called in a chopper."

"All right, Roz, you win," McBride said. "Send me directions. I can be there in an hour." He hung up. I quickly pulled up the instructions for getting to the cottage and emailed them to him.

"McBride's on his way," I said, grinning at my cat, who was sitting by the porch door, keyed up, peering out and hoping for a miracle. She swished her fluffy tail and shot me a look of disdain. We'd only arrived the evening before and I wasn't ready to let her out, but she was determined and I couldn't blame her. It was a paradise out there—teeming with birds and shrews, and myriad insects and other creatures.

I crouched down to scratch her ears as I looked out across the basin, where the helicopter had begun the process of dropping a man down. I stood and tried to see clearly as he found his footing on the sandbar. "Why don't I have fantastic binoculars like those cops had?" I asked the cat. She twitched her tail, and looked out through the glass again.

"Oh for heaven's sake—stunned or what? I've got my fancy new phone right here in my hand," I said, realizing that I could record what I was seeing to show McBride when he arrived. I moved the cat away from the door, stepped outside, and hurried across the grass to the cliff's edge, focusing on the distant action.

The lower section of the gnarled tree trunk was now well up on a pebbled sandbar and I recorded the progress as the fellow began to disentangle the girl's pale limbs from the dark roots. After several minutes, he had freed her and laid her carefully on the shingle. He walked a few steps away to pick up the rescue frame.

She was still wrapped in the flag. He had placed her on her side, her body turned towards the basin, her cheek cupped in the pebbles. I zoomed in, trying to get a clearer image of her, and was startled to see that her eyes were open, as though she was staring across the vast distance of the rapidly emptying basin—looking right at me. Yet so deathly still, her red hair strewn. But then the worker's legs and arms blocked my view as he knelt in front of her to secure her to the frame.

Within a half an hour, the whole of this remarkable undertaking was completed. Her body had been disengaged from the tangle of roots, tied onto the frame, and hauled up into the helicopter. Then the operator himself was smoothly hoisted back up. The chopper hovered for another moment, circled the basin, came directly overhead, and flew low along the bank following the strip of cottages. Then it abruptly turned right and I filmed it as it flew across the farmers' fields and disappeared over North Mountain. I stood stock still on the cliff's edge. I looked out again, across the basin. The girl was gone. I had the sensation of waking from a vivid dream.

What had sparked the RCMP's change in plans? They had no obligation to me, but I was irked at not being kept in the loop. I retrieved the card the corporal had given me and called.

"Corporal Monaghan," she answered.

"Hi, it's Roz. You were just out at my place on Longspell Road."

"Yup. What's up?" she asked.

"I'm curious about that recovery," I said. "Where do they plan to take her?"

"Once we get her into the Zodiac we'll take her into Wolfville and have her transported to the medical examiner's for an autopsy."

I was silent for a beat. "The Zodiac?" I said.

"Constable Cudmore's at the Wolfville detachment arranging to have one delivered to the Kingsport wharf ASAP." She took the tone of indulging me with information I already had and should recall. "But as we explained to you earlier, we'll have to wait for the tide before we can put it in the water."

"Tell Constable Cudmore he can scratch that arrangement," I said. "She was just removed from the Minas Basin in a helicopter."

Corporal Monaghan was silent. I proceeded to describe what I had seen in as much detail as I could muster. "I took pictures," I said, finishing my story.

There was a pause and then, "Why don't you forward those pix to my phone. There's something else I have to do out your way this morning. In the meantime I'll check this out." She hung up abruptly.

It was clear the RCMP were in the dark about the helicopter. Was this some kind of crossed-wire mix-up? If not, then who on earth had swooped in without informing the police?

This event called for a cup of tea—as the unexpected often does. I returned to the cottage and went through to the narrow kitchen and plugged in the kettle. It had now been the better part of an hour since my call to McBride and he'd probably take a cup himself when he arrived. He had been on the wagon for years and I worried that this recent upheaval with Sophie might drive him back to the bottle.

I paced around waiting for the water to boil, and then took my phone out of my pocket and sank into an old upholstered armchair in the enclosed porch and began to review the images I had captured. I had no idea how to forward photos from my new phone, but it was high time I figured out what most eight-year-olds could do in their sleep. The cat jumped up and settled herself on the arm, purring vigorously and watching me.

"Your charm and good looks will get you nowhere," I said. "You're not going out!" I was searching for identifying marks on the helicopter or the rescuer's outfit—logos, names, colours—but could see nothing on either the clothing or the gear. I was preparing to forward the pictures when the kettle finally whistled. I set the phone down on the arm of the chair and got up. The cat immediately batted at the phone and it slipped down between the seat cushion and the side of the chair and disappeared. "I saw that," I said to her, "and the answer is still no—cheeky!"

I poured the boiling water into the pot. It was a relief that the girl's body had been retrieved, but I felt anxious and out of sorts. I paced around the kitchen while the tea steeped. I stared at the mugs in the old wooden dish cupboard, and selected one.

I had been looking forward to going out by boat and examining how she was tied to the tree, having a close look at the flag and any other evidence that might have been overlooked and would now be lost forever. Not to mention getting the answers to questions like how long had she been dead, was she dead when she was first tied into the tree, and how exactly had she died?

I poured the tea, stirred in a little milk and a spoonful of the honey I had bought on the drive out the evening before. I moved through the porch and sat down on the wooden stoop, watching two hummingbirds argue as they hovered over a blossoming weigela by the corner of the house. I stared across the basin recalling what I'd witnessed.

I set the mug down as I heard the sound of a vehicle turning into the driveway at the front of the cottage. McBride had made good time. I was relieved that he was here—someone to share this surreal event with. I turned and looked at the cat, who was eyeing me intently through the panes of the porch door. "Molly's arrived," I said, teasing her. She blinked. Her scorn for the lab was evident. She looked up abruptly and I glanced around to greet McBride—but the two men in suits approaching me were strangers and they were moving fast. I got to my feet.

"No need to ask any questions, ma'am. Just know that we're here on official business, and to avoid trouble I would advise you to co-operate. You were observed taking pictures from this property this morning. We'd like you to hand over the camera or the device you were using."

"Sorry, did I miss the part where you identify yourselves?" I said.

"As I said, no questions." His tone was a little sharper. I looked at him curiously. Why, if this was official business, would he not show me his ID? I pushed back.

"Explain who you are and why I should hand my personal device over to you. It's legal to photograph the Minas Basin."

"Those pictures are now part of an investigation, so it would be wise for you to do as we tell you and hand it over. You can take this as a warning."

A warning? His lack of protocol and brusque manner brought out the devil, as my father used to say. Remembering that my phone had disappeared into the chair, courtesy of the cat, I decided to brazen my way through.

"When I was standing on the edge of the cliff taking those pictures, did whoever was observing me notice that I dropped my device? I'm afraid it may have fallen all the way down to the beach. I'm planning to look for it as soon as I finish my tea, but you're welcome to go on down now and start searching."

"Sure. We'll do that," he responded, "but we'll search the house first." He gestured to his silent associate who took a step towards me.

"Whoa! Not without a warrant, which you don't appear to have," I said. "And before you enter my house, I do have a right to have my lawyer present."

"Have it your way. We either take the device—or we take you," he said.

They moved in sync like lightning bolts, one to each side of me, and hauled me off the stoop. My foot knocked against the mug and my tea spilled over the step. I started hollering, but a hand was clapped over my mouth as they dragged me along the side of the cottage towards their dark-windowed Range Rover. I looked frantically around, but the road was deserted. The silent one got behind the wheel while the other shoved me into the back seat, got in, and forced my wrists together with plastic restraints.

"Don't speak," he said as the vehicle began to move along Longspell Road towards the highway.

We were almost as far as Longspell Farm's driveway when I recognized the red Subaru coming towards us. It was Ruby Sube—McBride's old wagon. I held myself back from a desperate attempt to yell or even to turn my head as it passed, for fear of giving away the fact that I had an ally in the neighbourhood.

We crossed Medford Road and continued on downhill to the junction, where Longspell met the main road coming out of Kingsport. Without warning, an RCMP car pulled directly in front of us, blocking our entrance to the highway.

"What the hell!" the driver said, rolling down his window.

I held my breath. What was this? Was I about to be rescued? But no—on the road coming out of town there appeared a bright red and yellow 1930s tractor followed by another, and then another. I watched the RCMP officer step out of the cruiser and give them the thumbs up. It was Corporal Riley Monaghan, grinning broadly as a long line of vintage tractors, driven by gleeful octogenarian collectors, pulled past her and began rolling in a proud cavalcade along the highway.

There were now three cars waiting behind us on Longspell Road. Our annoyed driver leaned on his horn and then abruptly got out of the SUV. Corporal Monaghan, keeping her eye on the slowly moving tractors, approached the SUV driver. "Sorry, sir. This highway is now blocked at all intersections while the Tractor Club's annual parade takes place. You'll have to wait."

"Let us through!" he said. "We're on important business here."

"This is important business too. You can easily turn around, go back to the Medford Road, and then cut over to Canning from further up. My guess is you'll likely beat the tractors into town—but no speeding now!"

The driver scoffed and turned back to the SUV. As he opened his door to get in, I lurched forward and shouted, "Riley!"

She turned as though she had heard something over the din of the tractors, but we were already on the move, screeching back up Longspell Road. My backseat companion grabbed me by the shoulders. "Another stunt like that and you'll be gagged!" he said pulling me roughly back into place.

"Look, who are you and what's going on?" I said. "What do you want with me?"

He was silent.

"This obviously has something to do with the helicopter," I continued. "Otherwise, why would you want the pictures?"

Still no response.

My mind was racing through my options. "Okay, you know what, I just remembered where my device is."

"About time," he said. Though he maintained a cold demeanor, I could sense his relief. He leaned forward and spoke to the driver: "She's decided to hand over the phone. We're halfway there—let's head back and get it."

I was banking on this. It would get me out of the vehicle, and with any luck McBride would be waiting at the cottage wondering where I was. Unless he had taken Molly for a walk. As we moved from pavement to gravel, I crossed my fingers.

Chapter 3

My backseat minder removed the wrist restraints and we got out of the car. He stared at McBride's station wagon. "Whose is this?"

"That belongs to the farm up the road," I lied impulsively, attempting to keep McBride a secret. "They park here when they're doing work at different places."

We walked around to the cliff side of the cottage. Molly stood and greeted me, wagging her tail vigorously. "Your dog?" the driver asked.

"No, no—she's from the farm, too," I answered. "She just runs free—runs around all over the place." I glanced through the large-paned windows. McBride was not in sight. But if Molly was here, he must be nearby. I opened the door and we stepped inside the porch—and they stood there, one looking at me expectantly and the other, the driver, looking out towards the basin.

"Okay, I'm going to track down that phone for you," I said, trying to sound contrite. I walked into the living room and slipped through the archway into the kitchen. Standing at the far end by the roadside door was McBride. I put my finger to my lips, walked right past him, and quietly pushed open the exterior door. "Let's go," I whispered.

McBride and I moved silently out of the house and ran across the grass to his car. I got in on the passenger side. "Hold on. Don't close your door yet," he said. He opened the back door behind me and bird-whistled softly for Molly, who came racing around the house and leapt into the backseat. He closed both doors at the same time, then jumped into the driver's seat and started the engine. With the enormous Range Rover blocking him in, he backed up a few inches, turned hard to his right, and drove rapidly across the yard, around a spindly red maple, and onto the driveway of the next cottage over.

Then we were out on Longspell Road and moving fast, McBride constantly checking his rear-view mirror. We were a couple of hundred yards down the road when I saw that incorrigible grin on his face. "There they are now," he said.

I turned to look. The suits were running along the side of the cottage towards their SUV. They didn't look happy. The road ahead of us curved to the left and I lost sight of them. Without warning, McBride abruptly turned right onto the driveway to the farm. At the top, he pulled in on the far side of an old grey Mazda truck, which served to mask us from the road below.

We got out and stood between Ruby Sube and the cab of the truck. There were three large barns, a farmhouse, several outbuildings, and plenty of laundry on the line, but there was no one around.

"So who are those characters?" he asked as we stared across the top of the cab and down to the road.

"You got me," I said, trying to steady my breathing. "They're not saying. They're after my phone—the pictures I took. They say its 'official' but they're behaving like thugs." I held out my wrists, which were bruised and scraped from the restraints.

"That's not your typical thug car. I think we're playing with the big boys."

"Speaking of…" I said, spotting the Range Rover as it came into view. We watched as it moved at a clip past the farm's driveway.

"Good thing farmers keep keys in their vehicles, eh, Roz? I'm guessing this one won't mind exchanging this little old Mazda truck for Ruby Sube."

"McBride!"

"Just for the morning." He was already around to the driver's side and getting behind the wheel.

"For God's sake, McBride, I'm renting a cottage from these people!"

"Don't just stand there with your mouth open, Roz. Get Molly and hop to it! No time to waste. Let's see what we can find out." He started the engine and put the truck in gear. I did as I was told. What else could I do?

Molly sat between us as we sped down the driveway and onto Longspell. Almost immediately we were at the intersection with Medford Road. "Turn right here," I said. "They'll assume we turned up this way to avoid the tractor parade—you must have just missed it, because you passed us when we were heading down towards the highway."

"Yup. The tractors were just lining up by the turn-off when I got here and I did see that SUV. Took a good look when I passed it because it seemed so out of place."

"Well, after the driver was turned back because of the parade, I told them I remembered where my phone was, hoping they would take me back to the cottage, which they did. I was counting on you being there. I figured you'd do something miraculous to get me away from them, and it worked because now here we are driving around in a stolen truck. I just hope they didn't find my phone."

McBride reached into his pocket. "This one?" he said, handing it to me.

"McBride! How did you find it...? What—are you psychic now? Did you catch that from Sophie?"

"How do you think I found it? I phoned you. Nearly gave myself a hernia!"

"You were in the chair! It was a trap set by the cat. I told her you were coming."

"Anyway, some disturbing pictures there, Roz. So who were you sending them to?"

"I was figuring out how to send them on to Corporal Monaghan—the Mountie who came out this morning and affirmed what I thought I was seeing. She had this Zodiac retrieval plan on the go, and was blindsided by that helicopter business, so she wanted me to send her—oh look! There's the SUV up ahead there, turning left by that yellow house."

"Weaver Road," McBride said when we got to the turn. We stayed well back, just keeping the roof of the SUV in view.

As they approached Pereaux Road, they surprised me by turning right. We followed suit and came over a rise just in time to see them turn left again.

"Where do you think they're heading?" McBride asked.

"Not a clue. Maybe they know we're behind them and this is a wild goose chase."

The road ended at the county highway, which led either down into the town of Canning or up North Mountain to the Look Off and beyond to Scots Bay on the Fundy coast. The SUV turned right and started heading up the mountain. There was plenty of traffic and we allowed several vehicles to come between us before we turned.

The long twisting climb ended at Gospel Woods Road on the brow of North Mountain. Most of the traffic in front of us headed right, towards the Look Off, a wide paved area off the highway that offered a stunning view of the whole valley. But the Range Rover didn't go that way. They took a short left and then a right onto Jasper Creek Road, a fairly straight and virtually deserted gravel road.

Following unnoticed would be impossible. We pulled over to consider our options before the turn. Just then, a large passenger van marked *Jasper Creek Centre for the Arts* passed us. Inside was a crowd of rollicking teenagers all talking at once. The van turned and began heading along Jasper Creek Road.

"Made to order," McBride said falling in behind it. The SUV was well ahead by now, moving fast, and kicking up dust.

A few kilometres along, the van signalled left at the sign for the Jasper Creek Arts Centre, and proceeded down a long driveway. But on the road ahead of us there was no SUV. It had completely vanished. McBride stopped the Mazda opposite the arts centre driveway and looked at me.

"We're pretty exposed on this road, but I think we should carry on, keep our eyes peeled, and try to find out where they went. They haven't turned off anywhere up to this point."

"I agree," I said. "Let's keep truckin'."

As McBride put the Mazda in gear, it sputtered, coughed, and the engine quit. He looked at the dash. "I'd say we're out of gas—that gauge never moved."

"Excellent choice of vehicle, McBride."

"We'll just walk down to that centre," he said. "I bet they have gas on hand. Maybe they can tell us what's further down this road. Come on, Roz. Molly could use the walk."

The lab bounded out of the truck delighted with this turn of events, finally getting the exercise she'd been craving. At the end of the long driveway there was an old farmhouse on our right, and straight ahead were parking lots and the main building. There was a sign for an art gallery and another for performance studios.

"Look at this place, McBride. They have studios! Maybe I can work on the Beckett stuff here."

"Uh huh," he said, glazing over as he always did when I mentioned my theatre projects.

We entered the main building and looked around for someone who might help us out. The teenagers we had seen in the bus were crowded around a reception counter where a blond woman was busily registering them one by one. Lingering at the back of the group was a tall kid with long green hair. I approached him. "So what's everybody up to?" I asked.

"Signing up for the animation workshop," the boy replied.

"Sounds cool," I said.

"Oh yeah, and you get a school credit for art class."

"That's excellent," I said.

I realized it would be a long time before the woman would be free to talk to us. I could hear the sound of a lawn tractor starting up, and looked back to where McBride had been standing, but he was already out the door and waving at the driver who had begun to mow around the farmhouse.

"Have a great workshop," I said to the boy, and stepped back outside. Molly had found herself an old tin basin filled with water and was drinking greedily from it. The young farmhand had stopped the tractor and was talking with McBride who was pointing to where our truck was stranded at the top of the driveway. The fellow got off the machine and he and McBride walked towards the drive shed. I followed. He was handing McBride a plastic gasoline container as I caught up to them.

"Hi, I'm Roz," I said.

The boy looked up and nodded at me. He looked about eighteen years old and he had intense blue eyes. What some might call sapphire blue.

"Do you happen to know if they rent out the performance studios here?"

"If they're available, they do. Call the centre and talk to Heather."

"Heather—okay, I'll do that," I said. "That's great, thanks."

"And what's further along Jasper Creek Road up there?" McBride asked, cutting to the chase.

"She goes right down to the Bay of Fundy. There's a few farms along the way, most of them deserted. There's a small quarry off to your right and then some summer cabins along the water. That's about it. But if you want to check out something awesome, I wouldn't bother with this road. Just over to the west you'll see a sign for Black Hole Road. Turn right and drive all the way down to the end. From there you can hike in along the brook. You'll come to a huge waterfall, and this steep gorge that opens right out into Black Hole Cove."

"You know your stuff," I said.

"I live out that way with my mother and sister."

"And you work at the centre here?"

"Just part-time, I lend a hand around the property."

"You don't happen to have noticed a big official-looking black Range Rover out this way?" McBride asked.

There was the briefest of hesitations. "You see a lot of vehicles over the course of a day. Listen, I better get back to this mowing."

McBride handed him a twenty for the gas.

"What's your name?" I asked.

"Jacob."

"We'll bring this container right back down to you. Thanks for your help, Jacob."

We headed out of the shed. As we walked past the farmhouse towards the start of the driveway, we heard a roar in the distance and could see a dust cloud speeding along Jasper Creek Road; it was coming from the direction of Fundy. We stopped in our tracks and I ducked behind McBride for cover. "Is it the SUV?" I asked him.

"Unless there's another one just like it." It thundered past the stalled Mazda without slowing down and continued on towards the highway. "They're still in a hurry," he said, as we watched the blur of dust disappearing.

When we finally reached the top of the long driveway, I leaned against the truck and groaned as McBride poured in the gas. The road was deserted. "Well, what now? We've lost them…twice."

"Since we're here, why don't we investigate further down this road anyway," McBride said. "We might find something."

"Or we could follow young Jacob's suggestion and go straight to Black Hole," I said bleakly.

"What do you call that, Roz—the karma of names?"

I shivered. A cold wind had come up, blowing straight in off the Bay of Fundy.

Chapter 4

MOLLY CHASED THE TRUCK DOWN the driveway when we returned the gas container to the shed, and then followed us all the way back up to the top. McBride stopped at the road to let her jump in.

"At least Molly's happy," I said as she settled in between us, panting. "Finally getting lots of exercise."

"The poor critter's been pent up in the house with me. But I'll tell you, she got some exercise this morning giving that cat of yours a run for her money," McBride said, chuckling as he put the truck in gear.

"What? You're saying the cat got out?"

"Oh yeah—I opened your door and she flew out of that porch like a tornado. Scared the bejesus out of me. Headed straight for the edge of the cliff with the dog on her tail!"

"McBride!"

"What?"

"For God's sake! We're definitely not going down to the end of this road. We're not going anywhere except back to Kingsport!"

"Roz, I'm sure she's—"

"No! We've lost those creeps for the time being anyway. We're heading back. Hurry up!"

We drove in silence down the steep winding road into the valley. I crossed my arms and stared straight ahead, trying to block out visions of all the disasters befalling the cat. As predicted, there was no sighting of the Range Rover.

We had just turned onto North Medford Road when the alarming shriek of a police siren cut into the silence. We pulled the truck over and the RCMP cruiser pulled in behind us.

"Well done, McBride," I griped.

"You're the one who told me to hurry! Besides, if it was up to me we'd be checking things out on the Fundy shore right now. This is your fault, Roz—"

"My fault! Did I let the cat out? Did I steal the truck?"

McBride rolled down the driver's window, and none other than Corporal Monaghan appeared.

"Can you show me your license, sir?" she said. "You know, I don't see an up-to-date sticker on the plate, so—"

"Corporal Monaghan," I cut in. "It's me, Roz, remember? I have to talk to you." I started to reach into my pocket to take out my phone.

"Just keep your hands where I can see them," she said sharply.

"Listen, this is important! We've been tracking these guys—they have something to do with the helicopter I told you about and—"

"I'm speaking with the driver of this vehicle right now," she said. "So cool it, or I'll have to restrain you and put you in the back of my car."

"I've already done that dance today, thank you very much." I wondered if, like Alice, I had fallen down a hole into a world where everyone was mean and contrary.

So far McBride hadn't said a word, but he was working up the charm. He handed Corporal Monaghan his driver's license. She took it from him and studied it.

"So how's that tractor parade going?" he asked, giving her his best smile.

She looked at her watch. "It'll be almost over now. I look forward to it every year. I've got a soft spot for those old guys." She smiled back at him.

"Salt of the earth," McBride said.

"The very best." She handed back his driver's license. "I need to see your registration."

"I have the registration for my car in here," he said, motioning to his wallet, "but my car is with the farmer down on Longspell. I borrowed his truck in exchange."

"That's not how it works," she said.

"No?"

"No. Because this truck isn't supposed to leave farm property."

"No! I guess I misunderstood."

"I guess you did," she said. "So, here's what I'm going to do. I'm going to follow you down to the farm and we'll get this truck back where it belongs, and we'll take it from there."

"Sounds like a plan," McBride said.

"In the meantime, your friend Roz can ride with me and fill me in on what's been happening since she took those pictures this morning." She gestured with a nod for me to get out of the truck.

"Okay, good," I said relieved, casting a glance at McBride.

"See you there," he said, giving me a big grin.

As we drove down Medford Road towards the farm, I told Corporal Monaghan about the two so-called official investigators arriving at my cottage in their armoured SUV and lifting me right off my own porch when I refused to produce my phone. "And you actually saw that vehicle and spoke to that driver," I said, "because he stepped out to give you a hard time when you made him wait for the tractors."

"Oh right. The cranky one."

"If cranky includes dangerous!—I was there! I was right there in the back seat with his partner who had put plastic restraints on my wrists." I held them out so she could see the marks. "Then, when I tried to get your attention, he threatened to gag me."

She was silent, so I continued with my story, telling her about returning to the cottage, discovering McBride by the back door and our hairy escape, how we hid his car at the farm, took the Mazda, and followed the SUV as far as Jasper Creek Road. "If we hadn't run out of gas up on North Mountain, who knows what we might have discovered. Something weird is going on, Corporal Monaghan," I said. "I mean, you saw that girl out there in the basin with your own eyes. Looks to me like abduction and murder—we don't know! And how did she end up out there?"

"Listen to me carefully," she said. "This is where your interest in this situation ends. There are some high-level conversations going on. Things are being looked after."

I was dumbfounded. "What sort of high-level?" I asked.

"That's not for me to get into—it's classified. But word has come down from the higher-ups that everything's being dealt with, and the smartest thing for you and your friend McBride to do now is forget about it."

"Forget about it? How do I 'forget' about my personal safety? Can you guarantee they won't be back to harass me? What's changed? I'm sure they're still interested in getting their hands on my phone!"

"You don't have anything to worry about. Admittedly, they were overzealous, and I'm sure they'll be reprimanded."

"Overzealous?" I said. "That's a hot one. Who are they? And who'll be doing the reprimanding?"

"Like I said, it's classified."

"Classified or not, I don't intend to look the other way. I'm going to charge those thugs with abduction!"

"Listen up, Roz, this is official! You're not hearing me. As far as you're concerned, this is over now. And here's what it comes down to: if you want me to give your friend McBride a break on helping himself to an unregistered truck and driving it all over the county, then you better cool your jets!"

She turned onto Longspell Road. McBride, who was just ahead of us in the Mazda, signalled and turned up the driveway to the farm. I was stunned.

"Let me out here," I said at the bottom of the drive. "I have to look for my cat."

"Don't forget to forward those pictures," she said.

I got out and stood for a moment watching the cruiser going up the drive. "Did that just happen?" I said aloud.

I felt as though I'd been hit in the stomach. I had made the mistake of assuming Corporal Monaghan was on my side. I had told her everything, and now I felt like a fool.

It's the first lesson of a good investigator: trust no one.

Chapter 5

I WALKED SLOWLY DOWN THE road, waiting for McBride to come along so we could talk about getting warned off the case. I tried to distract myself, lingering by the farmer's lush fields, well on the way with their spring crops. This is a painter's paradise, I thought. Van Gogh fields with North Mountain and Cape Blomidon as a backdrop.

I was checking either side of the road for the cat when a tall black and white tail swished through the high grass in the ditch to my right. I took a few steps over and caught sight of Mama and three baby skunks out for a promenade. I tried to recall remedies for skunked felines. Tomato juice, peanut butter, apple cider vinegar…oh yeah, she'd love that! If I found her.

I was startled to see a familiar van parked in my driveway. Walking around the cottage, I noticed that the four wooden Adirondack chairs had been moved and were set in a row facing out towards the basin. In those chairs, laughing and talking, sat Mark, Cym, Ellie, and Regan, the four performers in the Beckett troupe. Mark, lean and gangly, had his legs stretched out in the sun. Regan was lighting a cigarette, looking stern. Ellie, ever curious, was pointing at a hawk flying over the basin, while Cym, at the far end of the row, was on her phone, no doubt in yet another wrangle with her current girlfriend. Just then, Ellie turned and saw me.

"Hey, Roz! The whole Cat's-Astrophe has arrived!" The next moment, they were all out of their chairs and we were exchanging hugs. My spirits began to lift despite everything. "We thought we'd surprise you and drop out for a visit, have a bite and a natter about the Beckett stuff."

"I love that idea—but I have to tell you it's been one crazy day so far. I'm a little distracted. Speaking of catastrophes, is that the cat?" I looked in the direction of a strange yowling sound. "It is, isn't it? There she is!"

Two properties over was a cottage that had a towering ash tree in the centre of the garden. It had just begun leafing and was a real beauty. High up and clinging to a branch was the cat.

"What's her name?" Ellie asked me.

"You know, my friend McBride always teases me for naming my car but not my cat. I just call her The Cat, or You Again."

"And what do you call your car?" Ellie asked.

"Old Solid," I replied.

We hurried through the adjacent property and into the garden with the tree. I called up to her, but she wasn't budging. She was trembling, and her meow was pure pathos. I looked around. "No one seems to be here, no cars or anything, blinds are down."

"I don't see any ladders, but there's a rope hanging from that branch up there," Cym said. "Don't worry, Roz, we can get her." I protested, but there was no deterring them. The company were all in excellent shape—a physical theatre troupe with lots of strength and acrobatic skills. They got work gloves from their van and swung into action, standing on one another's shoulders until Mark and Cym were able to grab hold of the rope and pull themselves to the first major branch.

"Take the rope and swing it over that branch up there!" Mark said, tossing the end to Ellie. More climbing. Then Cym was within reach of the cat, though she was not exactly co-operating with her own rescue. In fact she was awkwardly backing up and a low growl was emanating from her. But Cym, in this as in all things, was undeterred. "Stand by, Mark. I'm going to hand her across to you," she said. "She's all claws—are you ready?"

"Standing by," Mark said. "Go for it."

Cym, precariously balanced on a branch, took hold of the cat by the scruff of the neck. She was lifting her over open space when we heard the sound of a car door slamming and Molly appeared, charging towards us, barking loudly. The cat began wildly squirming, and Cym couldn't get her all the way across to Mark but managed to get her near a stout lower branch. The cat clawed her way onto it and stared at the dog. Instantly ferocious and looking twice her size, she bolted down the tree and straight towards Molly who skidded to a halt, turned, and hightailed it back across both yards to McBride with the cat hot in pursuit.

"Hey, McBride!" I yelled. "Grab that cat and put her in the house!"

"I've done a lot of dangerous things, Roz, but I'm not doing that!"

I introduced the company to McBride. "This crowd all know Sophie," I said.

"Sophie and I have worked together a couple of times," Mark said. "She's up in Toronto, isn't she?"

"Auditioning right?" Cym said, checking her phone.

"That's right," McBride said.

"How's it going for her?" Regan asked.

"Not exactly sure. Haven't really uh…heard anything for a few days."

"Well, with auditions you never know—I mean, you never know until you know, and even then you don't really know, right? It's a crazy business," Ellie said.

"How about some tea?" I said, worrying that I'd put McBride on the spot by bringing up Sophie.

I managed to grab hold of the cat, and we all went inside. I put the kettle on. McBride called Molly into the porch and set down a bowl of water, which she slurped noisily. The cat scowled at this, quit the scene, and climbed up the built-in wooden ladder to the loft that extended over part of the living room.

"Perfect place for her," I said, watching her disappear.

"I'm going to take off, Roz," McBride said.

"You're going back to Halifax already?"

"Eventually. I should be there by sundown. Great meeting you all. Come on, Molly."

"I'll walk you out," I said, following him from the porch.

"Are you okay?" I asked him as we rounded the cottage.

"Never better. Are you?"

"Frankly, McBride, this all feels pretty bizarre. Did Corporal Monaghan tell you to forget about everything and back off the case?"

"In no uncertain terms."

"Well, I mean—what the hell? Something's up. Feels like some kind of outrageous cover-up is in the works."

"Well, that little warning she gave me was water off a duck's back."

I stopped walking. "You're heading back up North Mountain right now, aren't you?"

"Just a little exploring before I go back to the city. It's only early, and the days are long. I might find something...but I just want to get some exercise and clear my head."

"Be careful."

"Always. Oh and Roz, you can chill about the truck. I met the farmer—Jeffrey—very reasonable guy, didn't seem worried about it. In fact he thanked me for the gas, says he's run out a few times himself. I mentioned to him that you'd had some unpleasant visitors this morning and he wasn't happy to hear that, said he'd keep an eye out."

"That's good." I looked at him. "I should be coming with you."

"Take a break. It's your vacation. Enjoy your company."

"Let me know if you find anything," I said as he and Molly got in the car.

I watched Ruby Sube disappear down the road.

Just then, Cym came out of the cottage and headed towards the van.

"Did we mention we brought lunch?" she said, grinning. "We've decided to skip the tea and have the rosé we picked up at that winery down the road—it's awfully handy, isn't it? Have a glass with us, Roz."

"You bet I will," I said, trying to take McBride's advice and savour the fine company. "Let me help you carry in the lunch."

"The weather's so gorgeous—why don't we eat outside?" she said, lifting a hefty cooler out of the van.

"Of course that's what we should do." I grabbed the other end of it.

"And what a view. Look at that enormous beach—that tide must be all the way out now, is it?" she said as we set the cooler down on the cliff-side picnic table.

I looked out across the mud flats. There was the tree trunk, marooned on the distant sandbar, and I could so clearly envision the girl, tangled into the roots. "In fact, it's already turned," I said. "It will be high tide again just after seven tonight. Six hours and thirteen minutes each way."

"Wow, what an amazing place this is. Lucky you, Roz!" Cym said as she started to unpack the food.

"I'll go in and find some dishes for us," I said. I went into the porch and was about to announce that lunch was on, when my eye was drawn to something going on in the living room.

Mark, in the centre of the room, was standing on the square wooden chopping block that normally sat by the wood stove. His head was bowed, his arms at his sides, and he appeared to be trembling.

All at once I realized what was happening: they were re-creating the central image from *Catastrophe*, Mark playing The Protagonist; Regan, The Director; Ellie, The Assistant. I stopped still.

The Assistant, looking up at The Protagonist, standing head bowed on the plinth, says to the seated Director, "He's shivering."

The Director, smoking a fat cigar replies, "Bless his heart."

The actors stopped at this point and looked at me. Even without costumes or props, it was unsettling. The victim standing shivering on the plinth brought back the Abu Ghraib torture images I had seen on TV.

"That Beckett, just a tad ahead of his time, eh?" Ellie said.

"It's so simple, yet it speaks volumes," I said. "I was just starting to read *Catastrophe* this morning. We should seriously think about including this piece."

"Do you think Beckett wrote this because of the Second World War—wasn't he in the French Resistance?" Ellie asked.

"I know he worked for the Irish Red Cross," I said. "I plan to read about that while I'm here."

"I know something about *Castastrophe*," Mark said.

"Smarty-pants," said Regan.

"So what is it?" Ellie asked.

"Beckett dedicated it to Václav Havel," Mark said.

"A playwright—right? Czechoslovakia?" said Regan.

"Right. Havel founded the Committee for the Unjustly Persecuted. So, I think that's who this character is," Mark continued. "This abused and dehumanized man on the plinth is one of the unjustly persecuted."

Cym suddenly appeared in the porch. "How's it going with those dishes, Roz?"

"Oops," I said. "Fell down a well! Can you guys help carry out some glasses and forks and dishes? Lunch is out on the picnic table."

I didn't need to say more. Within five minutes we were set up outside in the early afternoon sun, diving into the feast they had brought with them.

"This is scrumptious," I said, chomping into yet another breaded artichoke heart. "You guys know how to do it up. Who made these?"

"Ellie did—fantastic cook!" Mark said. "On tour, she turns a tawdry motel room into a gourmet kitchen."

"How much time do you guys spend on the road?" I asked, spooning a large serving of curried shrimp salad onto my plate.

"Half our company's income is in touring," Regan said.

"And you're becoming so well known—didn't you recently perform for the Queen?"

"Today the Queen," said Mark, "and tomorrow a freezing band hall in East Bumblestick."

"Where the lights don't work," Regan added.

"And they forgot we were coming," Ellie chimed in.

"Touring is fabulous! Here's to touring!" Cym said, raising her glass.

"But at least now we have Beckett. And Roz, we love working on Beckett," Ellie said. "Because it's not just words—it's really physically demanding and disciplined. Right up our alley!"

After the meal we spent the next hour or so talking in earnest about building the show, where we'd like to tour it, and what festivals and other possibilities there might be in the offing.

I told them about the arts centre on North Mountain. "They have a couple of performance studios. Next week maybe we could spend two or three days working up there—and maybe even do an invited reading. Why don't I check it out for availability and costs and whatnot…what do you think?" I ventured.

"It's a great idea," Mark said.

"I think so too," Cym said. "I'd love to get away from the city!"

"Let's say, if you can get the studio for a reasonable rate, we'll do it," Regan said.

"And I still have this cottage next week. So, you could all stay here," I said. "There's plenty of space, and even the loft over the living room has a bed."

"Up where the cat went?" Ellie asked.

"That's right. In fact, I should go find the poor scruff and give her some lunch."

"She must be famished after that high-wire act," Regan said.

"Not to mention her Mad in Pursuit number," Cym added. "I thought she was going to knock me right out of the tree when she went after that dog."

I left them at the picnic table and went in through the porch to look for her. She wasn't in evidence on the main level so I climbed the wooden ladder up to the loft. It was possible to stand upright in the centre of the space, but the ceiling sloped steeply on either side. There was a made-up double mattress on the floor to my left and a small low window in front of me, which faced out to the road. I walked over, crouched down, and looked out. The front yard and driveway appeared calm and idyllic—no creepy SUV in sight. I sat back on my heels and looked around. Over to my left I spotted her. Just beyond the mattress she had compressed herself into a tiny notch of space where the floor didn't quite meet the wall. She was tucked down on the crossbeam that was lower than the floorboards. "Well, you're in a serious hiding-out mode," I said. "You look like a box of fluff."

I crawled onto the mattress and reached towards her. "Molly's gone now," I said, scratching her ears. "Why don't you come on out and act normal?" After a few moments of deliberation she got to her feet and stretched casually, stepped up onto the mattress, and immediately began washing her face and ignoring me.

From down below I heard Ellie calling me.

"Up here," I said. "Just found the cat—I'll be right down."

"We're going to pack up and head back to the city," she said. "Mark and Cym are washing up and Regan's outside smoking, but we're off in a few minutes. We've got a board meeting tonight, and by the time we get into town…." She was climbing up the ladder and her head now appeared over the edge of the loft floor. "Hey—this is cool," she said, taking in the space.

"So you guys arrive with a gourmet lunch complete with wine, and then you do the dishes too?" I said. "You're hired!"

"And don't forget we rescue cats!" She smiled, climbing up into the loft and sitting on the matress. "Hello, Pussycat, were you hiding?"

"She really was," I said. "See that tiny notch there between the floor and the wall—she was tucked in there."

"Good grief! How did you even manage to fold yourself in there?" Ellie said, peering at the tiny space. "Wait now, there's something else in there, Roz." She reached in and lifted out a little red book. "Could Pussycat be secretly writing her memoirs?" she said. "Are you?" she asked the cat.

"Maybe forgotten by a previous renter?" I said. "I'll take it up to the farm."

"Oh look, there's a name written here. Just inside the back cover." She handed the book to me.

"*This book belongs to: Aurelia*," I said, reading the sticker.

"Aurelia. As in phosphorescent sea animals, like moon jellyfish," Ellie said.

"Seriously, Ellie?" I asked. "Do you have a clandestine career as a marine biologist?"

"I wish," she said. "Gotta go!" She climbed down to the living room.

Chapter 6

I WAVED AS THE ACTORS' van pulled out of the driveway and the company began their journey back to the city. They gave a last holler and a little beep on the horn and I watched until they disappeared at the bend. The silence descended, and in the sudden quiet I felt apprehensive. Maybe I'll take my friend Samuel Beckett and go down to the beach for an hour or so, I thought. Back to where my day had begun. "I could use your company, Sam," I said aloud.

Intrigued by the earlier mention of Beckett's involvement in the Second World War, I decided to bring one of the biographies along and do a little research.

The newly found notebook was on the porch table and I tossed it into my bag along with the biography, my phone, and a large towel. The tide was now well on its way in, leaving only an hour or two of good beach time before it got too high.

I chose not to climb down to the shore via the apple ladders, and instead walked along to the end of the cottage road. From there, I could maneuver my way down through the rugged creek bed known locally as Ghoul's Hollow. There were some makeshift steps there and a handrail made of rope. Before I started down, I gazed across to the top of the next bluff over. There were several tall evergreens along the edge, some of which had their roots exposed through erosion and were hanging precariously over the beach. But the bluff was mostly pasture and the farmer's cows were peacefully grazing.

One by one, they looked up, stopped chewing, and stared across at me. I found myself smiling at them. Cows are a comfort, I thought as I climbed down through the hollow to the beach.

I walked along the mud flats back towards Longspell Point. I puzzled over how far this morning's fallen tree had travelled. Had it dropped from one of the bluffs nearby or had it journeyed all the way in from the Bay of Fundy through the Minas Channel and around Cape Blomidon? How long had that girl been out there, tangled in those roots? Again I felt vexed about not being involved in the rescue, not getting a real shot at finding out what had happened to her. And now, I'd had my knuckles rapped and been instructed to keep my nose out of the case altogether. I took strength from McBride's fearless response—"Water off a duck's back." He was incorrigible, and always an inspiration.

I found a smooth sandy spot, spread out the big towel, and settled in. I was on the other side of the point from where I had been that morning, and looking to my left I had a clear view of Cape Blomidon, luminous in the afternoon sun.

I took out the Beckett biography, used my rucksack and my sweater as a kind of headrest, and lay back on the warm sand. I consulted the index and opened to the account of the Normandy town of St. Lô, where two thousand of the twenty-six hundred buildings had been blown to bits during the Allied Invasions. It was a rubble heap when Beckett arrived as part of the advance team, and they were confronted with humanity struggling in the most basic survival conditions. The writer speculated that Beckett had signed on with the Irish Red Cross as his only means of getting back to France from Ireland, but Beckett proved a patient and conscientious asset to the unit. His fluent French was invaluable. He was appointed driver, quartermaster, and interpreter for the makeshift hospital. He secured the supplies and did whatever was required to help transform the rat-infested mud heap into a hospital.

To those who made it through, the horrific circumstances deepened their shared experience. For Beckett, it laid the creative ground for many of his dramatic and prose writings following the war, including the bereft characters in his play *Waiting for Godot*. His postwar writing ultimately won him the Nobel Prize in literature.

I closed my eyes, envisioning the shattered world Beckett had found himself in—so many clinging desperately to life, their anguished cries echoing through the night. I sighed, letting the book fall forward onto my chest. As I drifted, imagining the makeshift field hospital, I began to hear water rushing too, the sound drowning out their voices. I looked around for the source and in front of me, caught on a rocky ledge under a torrential waterfall, was McBride. I watched as he grabbed onto the branch of a tree that was protruding out of the cascade. He looked down to where a girl was tangled in the roots. He called out to her: "Hang on! I'll help—"

"It's too late," she cried, looking up at McBride as the branch was wrenched from his grasp and the broken tree slid down into the torrent, carrying the girl out into the waves, her red hair trailing in the sea foam. Then Molly began barking loudly, startling me. I gasped and looked around. But it wasn't Molly.

Standing there, staring down at me, was the woman I had met that morning—Grace. She had her two dogs with her and the large one was barking.

"Hey! Rosalind!" Grace was shouting. "Wake up!"

I looked at her in confusion.

"You better grab your stuff before it gets wet."

I lurched up to a sitting position, gaping around as the book slid from my chest onto the sand. The tide had lapped under my ankles and was moving fast. Grace bent over and quickly snatched up the book. I found my feet, rescued my towel, and pulled up my rucksack just as it was about to be submerged.

"We were on our walk along the cliff top. I could see you dozing down here with the tide moving in. I thought we better come down and warn you."

"Thank you, Grace," I said, looking at her in some amazement. "God, I fell sound asleep, that was stupid!"

"You're not the first. Are you all right?" she asked as we began making our way back towards Ghoul's Hollow. "I startled you."

"I was dreaming. So crazy how everything gets all mixed up together."

We clambered over the rocks and fallen branches and up the steps to the top of the bluff. Her dogs ran ahead. As we walked along and my head began to clear, I thought about bringing up the morning's events, to let Grace know that I'd been right, that what I'd seen hadn't been far-fetched after all. But something was holding me back from drawing her into it, an overall sense of peril—not to mention the warning I'd received from the RCMP.

"How's your stay going?" she asked.

"It's an extraordinary place, tide and all! I had a great picnic with some friends from the city earlier today. Where are you staying?" I asked.

"I live here year round. My husband and I have a house close to the beach down near the pier. He's been away, so I'm having some peace and quiet, but I'm picking him up tomorrow at the airport."

"What does he do?" I asked.

"He's a geologist, works over at the university. He loves it here, so close to the Bay of Fundy—it's a geologist's dream."

"But not many people live so close to Kingsport beach all year, do they?" I asked.

"This place is deserted in the winter and most of the spring. High summer's a different story with all the cottage owners in residence. They'll soon be here. But in the off-season we do meet the occasional renter like yourself, and the farm's a going concern year round."

We had reached the driveway to my cottage. "Here I am, safe and sound. Thanks again, Grace. You rescued me."

"Well, you were definitely in for a rude awakening. But I did save your book." She handed me the weighty biography and I wished her a good evening. She continued on down the road with her two dogs.

As I watched them go, my phone bleeped and I dug for it in my rucksack.

"McBride!"

"So I drove down Black Hole Road, Roz, hiked in alongside the creek and found those falls."

"Black Hole Falls?"

"Well, there are actually two waterfalls. The one I was at is right there by Black Hole Cove. It's called Haunted Falls, and like the young fella said, those falls are awesome—really high and roaring!"

"That's wild," I said, "because I just fell asleep on the beach and had a dream about you caught in a roaring waterfall... and the girl in the tree, she was there too."

"Climbing down from the top to get out to the cove would be no picnic. I didn't want to risk it with Molly. Another time I'll try approaching the cove from the beach side when the tide's out. And there are numerous caves along the shore that can be explored as well."

"I like that idea," I said. "Let's do it together."

"Maybe Sophie can join us. She texted me! She's flying in tomorrow. I'm picking her up at eight in the morning."

"That's fantastic news, McBride! You sound happy," I said, relieved that things might be resolving between them.

"It was nice to hear from her."

"Who are you kidding—you're beside yourself," I teased.

"Okay, I admit it. I can't wait to see her."

"You better get home and clean that house! Where are you now?"

"I was making my way back to the valley, but a few minutes ago I passed the turn-off to Jasper Creek Road where we were this morning, so I decided to check it out just in case. After this I'll head into Halifax."

"And what about the SUV?" I said. "Any sightings, or anything interesting?"

"Here's why I'm calling, Roz—I'm standing down here at the very end of Jasper Creek Road and right in front of me there's a disproportionately large industrial bridge that crosses this tiny creek that runs out into the ocean, and on the other side of the bridge a fairly new gravelled road leads up a steep incline and disappears into this dense forest right at the top which overlooks the Bay of Fundy. Got the picture?"

"I think so. End of the road, big new bridge, a steep hill, a forest at the top…."

"Right. If that SUV was heading anywhere along this mostly deserted road, it must have been here, and I can vaguely hear some kind of motor running up there. I don't have a clue what that could be. I'd like to find out, but strung across this industrial bridge in the middle of nowhere, there's a high-tech steel cable and signs that say *No Tres*—"

The phone went silent.

"What? *No Trespassing*?…McBride? Hello?"

I called him back, but no luck. If he had gotten out of range I knew he'd call me as soon as he could. I went into the cottage and poured myself a drink of water and fed the cat. But I couldn't shake the ominous feeling I had. Putting a *No Trespassing* sign in front of McBride was like waving a red cloth in front of a bull.

I went and stood in the porch and stared out at the basin. The morning's events washed over me. My gut instinct said, "Go immediately." I'd been dithering long enough. I grabbed a light jacket, got into Old Solid, and headed for North Mountain. There was still a reasonable amount of time before sunset. I pursued the same route we had taken that morning, only this time I would follow the road all the way down to the end. Hopefully I would arrive before dark and find McBride there or, with any luck, pass him along the way.

Twenty minutes later I was at the top of the mountain making the turn onto Jasper Creek Road. There was little traffic, but when I got close to the juncture with the arts centre driveway I was forced onto the shoulder by a huge tanker truck coming the other way. He blared his horn as he roared past me. Once the dust had cleared, I could see an older model silver-grey Honda at the top of the driveway. In the driver's seat was Jacob, the young fellow who had helped us out that morning.

I beeped my horn and waved to him. He turned right onto Jasper Creek Road and stopped. I got out and hurried across as he opened his window.

"Hi, Jacob," I said. "Roz. Do you remember me from earlier today?"

"Yeah sure, the gas."

"That's right. I'm actually out here looking for my friend—the man I was with. You haven't seen him by any chance? He would have a different vehicle. A Subaru wagon, red...."

"I've been working outside all day—he didn't come back to the centre."

"He followed your suggestion and hiked in to Black Hole Cove this afternoon. Said he saw Haunted Falls. Loved it!"

The kid nodded. "It's pretty cool."

"Anyway, he called me less than an hour ago from the end of this road. How far is it down to the Fundy shore anyway?" I asked.

"Ten K or so."

"He was telling me there was some kind of fancy industrial bridge there. But then we lost the signal."

"It's restricted."

"What is? The signal?"

"The bridge. Illegal or something."

"You mean—it's illegal to cross it?"

"Yeah, that's right. Listen, I'm running late for something—gotta get going," he said, putting his car in gear. "Just be careful when you go down there. Seriously. Don't cross the bridge."

I watched him drive away, towards the valley. I stood there in the lengthening shadows, overwhelmed with both apprehension and curiosity. How could a bridge in the middle of nowhere be illegal to cross?

Maybe McBride would have the answer by now. I got back into Old Solid and headed for the end of the road.

Chapter 7

I MUST BE ALMOST THERE, I thought. I'd been driving along the deserted road for what felt like forever. Now and again there were glimpses of the Bay of Fundy in the distance. The water glowed red in the low sun. I passed a hand-painted sign pointing to a small quarry off to the right. I recalled Jacob mentioning a quarry when we'd asked him about the road earlier in the day. A couple of kilometres closer to the water was a dirt lane going off to my left which appeared to run behind a line of summer cabins along the shore.

Abruptly Jasper Creek Road narrowed and I slowed to a crawl. It pitched down and then opened out to a small parking area edged by a couple of decrepit wooden fishing shacks which faced out to the rocky beach. There were no parked vehicles down there. I came to a halt on the brink of the slope. As I peered down into the deserted lot, the sun began to disappear below the distant horizon.

Nervous about negotiating the steep slope in the increasing gloom, I pulled over to the right as far as possible, parked, and began picking my way carefully along the incline on foot. Partway down, a wide, freshly gravelled road opened out to my right and I saw that it led to the oversized bridge McBride had called to tell me about.

I walked the twenty yards or so to the bridge. Strung across its entire width was the steel cable McBride had described. The cable was connected on either side to tall poles which sported metal signs reading: *No Trespassing. Violators will be Prosecuted—24-Hour Video Surveillance.* This was what McBride had been about to read to me when we lost the signal. I looked up. Atop the tall poles at either side were video cameras. Jacob's words came back to me. "Seriously: don't cross the bridge."

Had McBride crossed it? I checked the thick steel cable. It was automated and secured at either end, apparently requiring a code to operate, so there was no way he could have taken his car across unless someone had released the cable. The narrow little creek was several metres below the bridge, running out into the Bay of Fundy from the woods and dense brush of North Mountain. McBride had said that he could hear something running up on the bluff, but at this moment it was dead silent. Surely if he'd decided to duck under the cable and proceed on foot, his car would be right here somewhere. I whistled for Molly and called her name, but to no avail.

It was now dusk. I could only conclude that McBride had left the area prior to my arrival. Maybe his phone had simply died. Even putting aside Jacob's warning, it was getting too late for me to duck under the cable and climb the hill. I turned and began walking back up to my car. I scanned the parking lot and the beach beyond but could see no vehicles, no boats, no activity of any kind in the encroaching darkness. I got into Old Solid, reversed slowly, and managed to turn around. Relieved but confounded, I began heading back along Jasper Creek Road towards the Valley.

A couple of kilometres along the deserted road I felt compelled to give McBride's cell another try. I pulled over to make the call, but all I got was the exasperating "customer is unavailable" message.

This excursion had yielded nothing. I counselled myself to stop worrying about McBride. With Sophie coming home tomorrow, he was sure to be heading into Halifax by now. He was notoriously messy when left to his own devices, but I knew he'd be anxious to please her. Picturing him tackling his place made me smile. It would likely take him half the night to get everything in good order.

By the time I got back to my cottage on Longspell Road I was exhausted and hungry. The June bugs were slamming themselves against the windows, occasionally startling me and riling the cat. There was a heavy mist moving around the point, giving a damp chill to the night air. I heated up some Campbell's chicken noodle soup, and sliced some of the fresh bread the actors had left behind. I decided to make a little fire in the wood stove, grabbed a quilt from the bed, and curled up with my hot soup in front of the fire. I let myself get lost in a book my friend Harvie had sent me when I told him where I would be vacationing. It was Harry Thurston's *Tidal Life: A Natural History of the Bay of Fundy*. I began to relax, and told myself that all would be well.

A bright beam of morning sun came through the living room from the porch window, struck my eye, and woke me with a start. As I stretched out on the couch I knocked my rucksack over and its contents spilled onto the floor. I groaned and reached down for my phone to see the time. Almost nine. I had overslept.

I got to my feet, hauled the quilt from the couch, took it back to the bedroom, and went into the kitchen to put the kettle on. You Again was around my legs. I fed her, and returned to the pile on the living room floor.

I began placing the contents back into my bag—wallet, cosmetics, car keys, blood pressure pills. In the midst of it all was the notebook I had put in my bag the previous day so I'd remember to drop it at the farm. It had flopped open on the floor and was lying face down. As I picked it up, a small newspaper clipping fluttered out. I unfolded it. It had been cut out from the *Portland Press Herald*, a Maine paper, and was dated the March just past.

Young Journalist Wins Award

Portland's Aurelia Strange has won the Emerging Writer Prize for a national competition sponsored by the Society of Environmental Journalists. Her winning article is entitled "Our Lowly Honeybee Versus A Pesticide Giant." Ms. Strange graduated with honors from the King's College School of Journalism in Halifax, Nova Scotia, in 2012. In her interview, she said she hoped to use her prize money to take a trip back to Nova Scotia to work on a new investigation.

The kettle whistled and I jumped. While the tea steeped, I went into the porch and sat down in the big armchair with Aurelia's notebook. Inside the cover was a receipt for the book from a gift shop on Main Street in Wolfville. I flipped through. There was only one entry—she must have just begun to use it when she left it behind—it read:

Finally landed the perfect place to stay on the Fundy side of North Mountain—a great price and the little cabin is super clean and has electric heat. The woman is grateful to have a tenant for the place.

I'll be sad to leave this beautiful cottage, but I must get closer to the site & keep a better record of the daily activity if I'm going to make a watertight case. What I've *learned already is shocking. I believe I'm on the verge of a breakthrough and once I have all my ducks in a row, I will pursue an interview with the head honcho— treacherous though it may be. Will pack after I get back from the library and move up to the cabin later today.*

"Treacherous," I said aloud, staring at the journal entry and wondering what "activity" this young journalist wanted to be close to on the Bay of Fundy. And who was this "head honcho"? I set the notebook down and went into the kitchen to pour the tea. As I was stirring in the honey, my phone rang.

"Hello—yes? Hello!" I caught it just before it went to message.

"Roz?"

"Sophie! McBride told me you were flying in this morning. How are you?"

"Upset is how I am. Where's McBride? My plane was right on time. I arrived over an hour ago. I've called his place, called his cell…no sign of him. So where is he, do you know? Roz? Are you still there?"

"I'm here, Soph…God, I don't know what to tell you. I'll drive in and get you."

"No, no, I'll grab a cab. It's fine, thanks—I'm just…I was determined to make things better between us. Fresh start, right? He promised to be here and he's not. I feel like a total loser."

"Look, Sophie, McBride was over the moon that you were coming home. He told me he'd be picking you up at 8 this morning. Whatever's happened, it's my fault. I've dragged him into this bizarre situation that came at me out of the blue yesterday. When he left my cottage, he wanted to do a little on-the-ground investigating before heading to Halifax. I better go, Soph…I've got to track him down. I'll find him."

"Well, don't leave me in the dark, Roz! Call me to let me know what's happening." We rang off.

I was shaking. I had to calm down and think clearly about this. McBride had been in sticky situations many times before, and emerged without a scratch. But I had just told Sophie I would find him, and I had no idea where to look.

Chapter 8

By 10 a.m. I was back on Jasper Creek Road, where my search for McBride would have to begin. As I passed the driveway to the arts centre, I impulsively turned in to seek out Jacob. I wanted to find out if he knew more than he had told me about the industrial bridge and why it was so heavily secured.

I drove down past the farmhouse and the outbuildings. He was nowhere to be seen, but as I reached the parking lot by the arts centre entrance, the door opened and the woman I had seen registering students the previous day came out.

I called out to her. "I'm looking for Jacob! Is he around?"

"I think he's stacking square bales for an outdoor benefit we're doing in the field this weekend," she said, walking towards the car. "And you are…?"

"I'm sorry," I said, realizing how anxious and rude I must seem. "I'm Roz." I stepped out of the car. "Are you Heather?"

"Yes, I am," she said.

"Jacob mentioned you to me," I said. "I'd asked him whether you rent studio space—I'm looking for something for three days next week."

"Wednesday through Friday is available."

"Really?"

"You're in luck," she said. "After that, both studios are booked solid with rehearsals for our own productions, so you just squeaked in."

"I'll take it." I got out my cheque book to give her a deposit.

"Don't you think you should take a quick look at the space first?"

"You're right," I said, trying to focus. If I didn't find McBride there was no way I'd be able to switch gears and work in the studio the following week. But maybe the company could use the space and do the work without me.

She walked me through the studio. It was perfect, and I told her so.

"What will you be working on anyway?" she asked.

"Beckett material—short works. Myself and four actors from Halifax are starting to put a show together."

"What brought you out here?"

"I was driving around these parts with a friend yesterday and I'm embarrassed to say we ran out of gas. That young fellow—Jacob—helped us out. I don't see him here today. I might track him down just to say hello."

"Feel free. Just out behind the red barn next to the main building."

"Thanks, Heather," I said as I hurried out the door.

"I love Beckett," she called after me.

"Me too."

Following her directions, I took the path to the field behind the barn. Sure enough, there was Jacob moving bales and rustic wooden benches to create a presentation area.

"Hi, Jacob." He nodded at me as he set a bench in position. "This looks nice," I said. "I just met with Heather. I'm renting a studio here for a few days next week."

"That's cool. So did you find your friend last night?"

"No. Have you seen him today by any chance?"

He shook his head. "Nope."

"You know how you warned me against crossing the bridge?"

"Yeah."

"Well, I didn't cross it."

"Good."

"But I'm thinking maybe McBride did—he's just that kind of guy."

"He would have been stopped. They don't fool around."

"You sound like you have first-hand experience."

"You hear things. Anyway, you're better off steering clear of it."

"What's up there on the other side of that bridge anyway?" I asked.

"Guard dogs for one thing—German shepherds. And not the friendly kind."

"So, say they did find him crossing the bridge, what would they do? Have him arrested?"

"I'm not sure. Really sorry, but I got a lot to do here."

"It's just—I mean—it isn't like my friend to disappear. He was supposed to pick someone up at the airport today, and he didn't make it. So now I'm on my way back down to the end of the road again. I don't know what else to do. I have to keep looking. Can you think of anything I should know, or is there someone up there I could contact by phone—anything at all…."

"Look, I'd like to help you but I really can't." He walked away from me and picked up a large square bale. "Just be careful, okay?" he shouted over his shoulder.

∞

It wasn't yet eleven o'clock and the sky was very bright. As I drove along I was getting a much better look at everything than I had on the previous evening. The road was not heavily populated or developed. There were a couple of small working farms, but many buildings were abandoned and in a state of decline. Once again I passed the handmade sign across from the quarry, and made a mental note to check it out on my way back.

The steep incline at the road's end did not look nearly as formidable or treacherous as it had the night before. There was a blue Ford pickup truck parked in the little open lot by the two fishing shacks, and I decided to drive down and see if there was anyone around that I could talk to.

I passed the turn that went off to my right towards the oversized bridge. I continued slowly down the steep slope. Old Solid proved her worth and I parked facing the glorious Bay of Fundy. The tide had begun to go out and there were all manner of ancient-looking rock formations, large pieces of driftwood, and stones of all shapes and sizes on the rugged beach.

I got out of the car. There was a light breeze and it was brisk, but the sun was climbing in the sky and it had the promise of warmth. I moved to the front of my car and stared out at the water. I looked to my right at the part of the Bay of Fundy known as Scots Bay. There the land curved around like a giant fishhook and then narrowed into Cape Split, with the sharp end of the hook projecting out into the bay. Across the water from where I stood was that dramatic rocky end point, and beyond Cape Split was the Minas Channel and the Parrsboro shore. The landscape had a mythic glow in the morning light.

I was startled by a voice: "Where you from?"

I turned. There was a ruddy-looking older fellow in a plaid jacket standing by the pickup. He was gaunt with piercing eyes and prominent cheekbones. He was scrutinizing me from under the bill of his peaked cap.

"Halifax," I said.

"Just a gawker then?"

I couldn't help but laugh at this assessment. "It's worth gawking at, don't you think?"

"There's lots do, so it must be."

"Do you live around here?" I asked.

"Just back the road a piece."

"What's the story with the fancy bridge?"

"The old bridge was done for, so they built a new one."

"But why is it restricted like that? What's up there? Why is it so big?"

"Nosy parker, are ya?"

"Can't help myself. Just curious."

"Private interests, best stay out of it."

"But what's up there—is it a business or a factory or what?"

"If they'd a wanted you to know, they wouldn't have put that big steel cable acrost it, now would they?"

"But you must know—I mean, if you live here."

"I know enough to keep myself to myself."

"What would happen if I crawled under that cable and walked up that road?"

"Best advice—when you're done lookin' out at the water here, take a run over to Halls Harbour, buy yourself a lobster for dinner, and head on back to the big city."

There was a no-nonsense edge in his voice that unnerved me. "Sounds good," I said. "I'm just going to take a walk along the beach first."

"Best go that way." He pointed west, away from wherever the bridge led.

I glanced the way he pointed, towards the cabin frontage. "There don't seem to be many vacationers around," I said.

"Well, you know what they say...."

"No. What do they say?"

"Two seasons. Winter and July."

"That explains it," I said.

I locked my car and climbed down from the parking lot onto the rocks, and started to pick my way along the beach. I found a large flat rock and sat on it looking out. After a couple of minutes I looked back at the lot. The man's blue truck was still there but he was nowhere in sight. Perhaps he had gone inside one of the shacks. Something had prevented me from asking directly whether he had seen McBride—it was a sense that if I did, I'd be putting myself in danger.

I decided to keep walking.

I continued following the beach as it curved inward and the next time I glanced back, I could no longer see the parking lot. I found myself alone in the quiet wilderness between the rocky shore and the Bay of Fundy.

I stood still and looked into the distance, trying to focus my attention on McBride. When he'd called me the previous evening, he had been right at the end of Jasper Creek Road, looking at the bridge and describing it to me. Would he have clambered under the cable and walked up the steep gravel slope and into the dense spruce forest at the top? Was he then "stopped," to use Jacob's word, and taken somewhere? That seemed the most likely. They had him—whoever they were. And if he had proceeded on foot, where was his car? Or had they let him through, car and all? And was there a connection between this bridge and my abductors in the SUV whom McBride and I had followed onto this very same road? If so, then there must be a link between McBride's disappearance and the girl in the tree.

It seemed I had no choice but to find a way to the top of that towering cliff and suss out what exactly was going on up there. If I were to follow the creek away from the coast and back into the dense brush I'd likely find a narrow place to cross it. Once across, I could come back towards the coast along the other side of the creek and then climb up to the ridge without being detected.

I decided to try it.

I began to pick my way back along the beach, towards my car. When I was just about in front of the parking area, I was distracted by a strange whining sound. Some distance along the shore below the high-forested ridge, I could make out the shape of something black moving among the rocks.

I stopped in my tracks.

I did my best to imitate McBride's special whistle for Molly. The creature responded, though its movements were awkward. But it was her! I was sure of it. She was half-whimpering, half-barking as she began to make her way towards me. She was noticeably injured, and I was afraid she would hurt herself even more clambering over the sharp rocks.

I tried to get to her as quickly as possible, but it was slow going for me too. A broken ankle wouldn't help anyone at this point. I glanced toward the parking lot but there was no sign of the old coot.

I tried calling softly: "That's okay, Molly—that's okay. Take it easy."

Finally she was within my reach. I crouched down to get a careful look at her. She licked my face—never my favourite thing—but I was so overwhelmed with the emotion of finding her that I was all tears as I examined her. She had a nasty open wound on her right haunch. Could it be a bite from the guard dogs Jacob had mentioned?

I wondered how she had ended up on the beach. Had she come down from the top of the cliff? It was a precarious drop.

If she had fallen, even from partway down, she could well have internal injuries.

"Can you walk, Molly?" She had a limp but came painfully along at my side. We climbed slowly up from the rocks onto the flat parking area. I dug for my keys and opened the passenger door of Old Solid. I reached over the seat into the back, grabbed a towel, and spread it out. "Can you climb in?" I patted the passenger seat. She looked at the seat and then at me. I bent down and gingerly lifted her into the car. If only she could talk!

Once she was still I moved hastily around to the driver's seat, turned the car around, and began to drive up the steep climb to Jasper Creek Road, keeping the car in low gear.

I got onto the road proper and drove fast. I needed to get this dog to a vet.

Chapter 9

As I was passing the driveway to the arts centre, I could see Jacob cutting brush along its upper ditches. I braked abruptly and pulled over to get directions to the closest vet. I jogged the several yards down to where he was. He glanced up at me, but didn't say anything—just pointedly kept working.

"I don't mean to pester you, Jacob," I said, "but I've got an emergency and I need your help."

"What is it?" he asked with a tone of stoic patience, his eyes on his task.

"I just found my friend's dog, Molly, down on the Fundy shore and she's badly injured. I think she fell—or was thrown down from the cliff top. I need to know where to take her."

His restrained attitude dropped away and he looked at me.

"She's in your car?"

"Yes."

"Let's have a look." We walked rapidly up to the top of the driveway.

I opened the passenger door and Molly attempted to wag her tail, but she was clearly suffering. Jacob leaned in and looked at the bloody wound on her haunch. He moved his hands gently over her rib cage.

"I don't feel any broken ribs," he said. "Maybe she's just badly bruised. But this bloody gash needs treatment right away."

"Does it look like a bite to you?" I asked.

"It could be, or maybe a cut from a jagged rock. I can't tell. I'd take her right down to Wolfville. I know them, they're good." He gave me clear directions to the vet's office. "You'll be there in less than half an hour," he said.

"Thank you, I really appreciate this," I said. He carefully closed the passenger door as I hurried around to the driver's side.

"So you found the dog—but not your friend?" he said, just as I was about to get into the car.

"That's right," I said. "I'm completely beside myself about it."

"Maybe you should report him missing," he said. "You could do that while you're in Wolfville."

"You're right," I said, thinking about how McBride was in this fix precisely because he had defied the RCMP's warning.

∽

I broke the speed limit and was crossing the Cornwallis River in just over twenty minutes. After one look at Molly, the veterinarian took her for immediate examination. "Wait here," he said. I paced around in reception for a few moments and then decided to call Sophie.

"What's happening, Roz? I'm going nuts," she said.

I explained that I hadn't yet located McBride. "But Sophie…" I paused to get a grip on myself, "I've found Molly."

"Oh, God. Is she dead?" Sophie asked.

"No, but she's seriously injured. I'm in Wolfville. The vet's with her now. I'm not sure whether she's going to make it."

"I'm coming out there, I'll be on the next bus. I've already checked—it gets in at three o'clock."

"I'll pick you up."

I was relieved. Sophie had been my anchor on many occasions. I knew she'd be a mess now with McBride missing, but we would help each other through this—whatever happened.

The vet's young assistant came out from the back, said it would be a while before they could fill me in on Molly's condition, and suggested I go for a coffee. I stepped out onto the street. I had a couple of hours until Sophie arrived.

I was hesitant about talking to the police, but with nowhere to turn I decided to take Jacob's advice and pay a visit to the Wolfville detachment. I walked down Main Street and went into the station.

"Does Corporal Monaghan work here?" I asked at the desk.

"She's out on a call. Would you like to see someone else?"

"Any idea when she might be back?"

"Impossible to say. Could be any time. Or if she's tied up with a case, we may not see her until tomorrow."

"Can I leave a message for her?"

"You can leave a message on her phone." He gave me her card.

I was back to square one. I already had her card. But just as I was leaving the building, I spotted her pulling into the parking lot. Okay, I thought, it's meant to be.

I walked over to her car. She looked up at me and smiled. "Hi, Roz, how are you?" Like we were old friends.

"Not the best," I said. "Can we sit down and talk? I need your help."

"Let's go in."

We settled into an interview room. She asked me if I wanted a coffee.

"I'm fine, thanks," I said.

"Okay. What's up?"

"I'm in town because I had to bring McBride's dog to the vet."

"I see."

"After we saw you yesterday, McBride went back up North Mountain to do a little investigating."

"I officially warned both of you to keep your noses out of this case."

"I know you did, but he was alarmed by the day's events. McBride is a stubborn guy and an experienced investigator and now he's disappeared."

"So, you're here to report a missing person."

"He's definitely missing. He was supposed to pick up his wife at the airport this morning and didn't show up. But this is more than just missing. McBride called me yesterday shortly before sundown to say that he was standing in front of the security cable that goes across this industrial bridge at the end of Jasper Creek Road. Do you know the place I'm talking about?"

"I haven't seen it but I know where you mean."

"Well, it's at the end of the exact same road we'd followed the SUV onto earlier in the day. Anyway, either we lost the phone connection or something happened to him right when he was talking to me. In any case our call was interrupted and that's the last I heard from him."

She didn't look convinced. "The cell phone signal up that way is sporadic at best. It's not unusual."

"There's more. When I found out he didn't make it to the airport this morning, I went down Jasper Creek Road to look for him. What I found was his dog, Molly, badly injured, and crawling over the rocks. She has what could be a very nasty bite, and someone told me there are a couple of unpleasant guard dogs up there beyond that bridge. Possibly she was thrown down, or chased and fell from the top of the bluff onto the beach. The short of it is, I've worked with McBride for a long time and he's not an amateur. He would have found a way to contact me by now if he could. I know he's in danger, and we need to get on this now. I need your help. It's an emergency."

"You say someone told you there were guard dogs. Did you see any?"

"No."

"So you found McBride's dog on the beach?"

"That's right."

"How do you know there wasn't some kind of water mishap? Maybe the dog went into the water and McBride tried to save her—or the reverse. That shore is notoriously rough. Or possibly he went exploring off-road and ran into trouble. The woods are thick there—there are creeks and bogs and fallen trees. If, as you say, it was sundown it would be easy to get lost and disoriented. It's not uncommon."

"That's not what happened."

"You don't know that. You're surmising based on suspicions you have—but you don't have real evidence to back them up. It hasn't even been twenty-four hours right? It doesn't qualify as an official missing persons case yet."

"Look, I'm asking you to go out there and check it out. There are cameras at that bridge—can't you examine the surveillance footage? Can't you look for his car? It's a red Subaru wagon."

"When I get a chance I'll take a run up the mountain, but not before the twenty-four-hour period has elapsed."

"Listen, Corporal, I didn't make up the events of yesterday. That girl out there wrapped in the flag, the helicopter, my bizarre abduction in an unmarked SUV. McBride and I didn't just imagine that same vehicle turning onto the Jasper Creek Road—that's all real. Something's going on!"

"You need to calm down. And by the way—you never sent me those photos."

"How do I know they won't be used against me?"

"I'd just like to see them."

"I'm still figuring out how to use my new phone."

"I thought you were a professional."

I stood up. "So you'll be in touch after you've checked into it?"

"If I find something, I'll let you know. Thanks for coming in, Roz."

∽

Shoot me! I thought as I left the station. I went down the walkway and stood for a moment on Main Street. Suddenly my eye caught on something: just across the street and down a bit was the gift shop where the notebook had been purchased. And I still had time to kill before picking up Sophie.

I went into the shop and removed the book from my bag and took out the receipt. I walked up to the counter.

"I've just found this journal and I'm trying to track down the person it belongs to," I said to the woman behind the cash. "I'm wondering if you remember selling it."

"May I see?" she asked. I handed her the notebook. It had a red leather cover and was very well made. There was a slender ribbon that could be used as a page marker. She opened the back cover and saw the name inside. "Aurelia," she said. "Unusual name."

"Yes," I said. "Do you remember her?"

"You know, we don't sell a lot of these little notebooks because they're pricey and the students can't afford them. But I think I remember having a conversation with this girl. I believe she said she had won a prize or something and was treating herself to a new daybook."

"That's right, she won a journalism award. You have an excellent memory. Can you recall what she looked like?"

"Well, let's see…she was about your height—maybe a little shorter. It was a chilly day so she was wearing a dark wool hat, but her hair was long. Long red hair—I remember that, but I don't think I've seen her since then."

"Red hair?" I said. "Are you sure?"

"Yes. And blue eyes, I think. That pale Celtic look, you know…."

My mouth was suddenly dry.

"I do know that look," I said.

"Are you okay?" she asked. "You look like you've seen a ghost."

"Thanks for your help…I'll try and…get the book back to her."

I walked out and stood stock still on the pavement. Were they one and the same, the pale, red-haired Aurelia and the girl in the tree?

Chapter 10

Sᴏᴘʜɪᴇ ᴡᴀs ꜰɪʀsᴛ ᴏꜰꜰ ᴛʜᴇ bus, and with barely a greeting we headed straight to the vet. He came out from the examination room to fill us in. He had disinfected and bandaged Molly's wound and confirmed that it was indeed a vicious bite, which had become infected. He had taken x-rays to make sure her bones were not broken and though they looked good, he wanted to study them in detail as Molly was badly bruised. She was sedated and they were now in the midst of re-hydrating her. He thought she should stay in the hospital for at least another day so he could change the dressing and observe her recovery, make sure her kidneys were functioning, and see if she could take food.

"She has definitely suffered serious physical trauma. I've seen these kinds of injuries go either way. We'll know more in twenty-four hours." He excused himself.

"I'd like to see her," Sophie said to the assistant. "Just to lay eyes on her for a minute." She nodded and Sophie followed her to the back room.

In no time at all she was back. "Molly's going to be okay, Roz," she said. Sophie was so often right about what the future held that her certainty about Molly's recovery was a comfort.

We got into Old Solid and headed for Kingsport. I filled Sophie in on the events of the previous day—McBride and I pursuing the SUV until we ran out of gas, the young fellow at the arts centre, Jacob, coming to our rescue, and then McBride heading to the mountain on his own. Then I told her about this morning's trip down to the Fundy shore that led to my discovery of Molly. Finally, I recounted my recent discouraging encounter with Corporal Monaghan.

"I think we should jump on your idea to find another way up to that bluff. If that's where you think McBride is—what are we waiting for? Let's go now."

"It will take a little research first, Sophie. I'd like to get my hands on some kind of detailed map. I mean, we don't want to wind up missing as well."

Just as we were approaching the village, I remembered Grace telling me that she lived near the pier—and that her husband was a geologist.

"Geologists have maps, don't they?" I asked Sophie.

"Beautiful maps," she said. "I went out with a geologist from Denmark several years back—Björn, his name was. He had maps—lots of them! He would show me where things came from, what era was represented. Björn's training crossed over into archeology too. He was always taking off to ancient sites around the planet."

We'd been driving through Kingsport, and I pulled onto the wharf. The canteen had just opened for the season and there were a handful of people lined up for ice cream and hot dogs. I parked alongside the boardwalk. The tide was well into its return. Sophie grabbed her shawl from the back seat and walked along the pier, looking out at the Minas Basin while I went to talk to the girls working the canteen.

"Hi," I said. They appeared to be twins, with identical long dark braids. "I'm looking for a woman named Grace; she has a two dogs, a big one and a little one."

"Oh. I know who you mean!" said the first twin. "Grace Stevenson. She was just here a while ago, coming back from her walk."

The other twin picked up immediately. "Her house is just up the road there, the second house along. And it's Sorensen, not Stevenson," she said with a sidelong glance at her sister.

"It's that place where they cut down all the maple trees," added the first twin.

"Elms," said the second.

"Thanks, girls."

I crossed over to the boardwalk and filled Sophie in. "I met a woman on the beach yesterday. Grace. She's married to a geologist. Let's see if they're home. I'll leave the car here for a bit."

We walked away from the wharf and started up the hill. As we came to the second property, I could see all the wide tree stumps in the yard where the elms had been cut down, probably stricken years earlier with Dutch elm disease. We passed the honeysuckle hedge that bordered the road and turned into the driveway.

Before we got to the door, Grace came around the side of the house carrying some freshly cut early lilacs. "Rosalind!" she said, surprised. "How are you today?"

"Fine thanks, Grace," I replied. I introduced Sophie and then got to the point.

"You mentioned that your husband is a geologist, and I wondered if he had any detailed maps of North Mountain. Sophie and I are interested in hiking up there."

"He has loads of maps—but you'll have to ask him. We have an understanding: I don't go into Björn's study, and he doesn't spread his rocks and papers all over the house. He's out at the moment, a meeting at the university. Come back in an hour or so. He should be here by five."

"Thank you, we'll do that," I said. "See you then."

I couldn't look at Sophie until we were back on the road. "Björn?" I said.

"Oh my God. How weird is that?" she said.

"Maybe all geologists are named Björn."

"If it turns out their last name is Sorensen, it's him."

"It is, Sophie. At least according to one of the twins. Are you okay with seeing him?"

"It was years ago, Roz. I'm not a teenager. I'm sure we'll be pleased as punch to see each other. In fact, I'm curious to see how the years have treated him."

"Let's drop your stuff into the cottage and have a cup of tea. The thing is, by the time we've visited Björn and studied the map it may be too late to go through the woods tonight. We'd be caught in the dark."

"We'll get an early start tomorrow then."

I was buoyed by her determination to keep her spirits from crumbling. "I'm so relieved you're here, Soph," I said.

"How are you doing anyway, Roz? Liking the new job?" she asked as we turned onto Longspell Road and headed towards my cottage.

"I do. It's amazing to actually have steady income, and about time, too. God, I'll be forty soon. The truth is, though, Sophie, I felt like I really needed this vacation because I'm trying to cheer myself up—change focus, get back to some theatre work. It's just…sometimes the job really gets to me."

"How do you mean?"

"So many of the crimes we prosecute are because of corruption and exploitation of resources. The more I learn working on environmental cases, the more the grim truth sets in. All these corporations and companies just want to keep making a buck, no matter what. Some of these CEOs really are sociopaths—the lengths they'll go to get around regulations is mind-boggling. They'd sooner pay a huge fine and keep profits coming in than actually preserve the planet for future generations—their own children for God's sake. It's very disturbing. Anyway, I needed a break from it."

"What about that prosecutor, Harvie? Are you guys still seeing each other, or did he take that job?"

"He did. He moved to Montreal last month, not long after you left for Toronto. We're in touch from time to time. I think he's happy with the decision."

"So you two weren't serious?"

"Actually, I think we're still crazy about each other, and we'll always be really good friends, but basically we're loners, and for both of us, work comes first."

"At least you're fighting the good fight, Roz—like you always do."

"If it's not one thing it's another, right? Who would have thought I'd be spending my first real vacation looking for McBride," I said as we turned into the driveway at my cottage.

∽

An hour later we were back at Grace's. This time there was a car in the driveway—a green Volvo wagon.

"Are you ready for the old boyfriend?" I teased Sophie.

"No time like the present."

We parked on the roadside and walked up the drive. The front door opened and there stood Björn. He was a tall, fairhaired man with a warm smile.

"Oh my goodness, a face from the past!" he said, with his slight Danish accent. "Wonderful to see you, Sophie."

"Isn't this unbelievable, Björn? I had no idea you were living in Kingsport."

"I see your name in the paper every now and again when you're doing a play," he said, "and I watched you in that science fiction series on TV. You had a fairly gruesome death as I recall."

"Yes—an unseen force pushed me down the stairs. It was too bad they killed me off, that was a good gig."

"Well, perhaps the Master of the Void can bring you back to life. Or maybe you now could join that zombie series, and become one of the walking dead."

"Excellent idea! I'll tell my agent," Sophie said, laughing. "This is my friend Roz—Björn."

"Nice to meet you," I said, shaking his hand. "I understand from Grace that you're a geologist."

"Yes, and she mentioned that you two are looking for some maps."

"We'd like to get the lay of land up by Jasper Creek Road and that vicinity around the Bay of Fundy."

"It's a very rich area there—lots of amethyst and agate, jasper of course. Are you looking for something in particular?"

"Just exploring," I jumped in, wanting to keep our concerns about McBride to ourselves for the time being. "Do you know how far back into the bush Jasper Creek runs?"

"I can loan you a couple of maps that are very precise. One will show the topography, the creek and the bogs and so on. And the other will show you the geological properties. Please, come in, come in. Grace is not at home. She has started a watercolour group and the few that live here year round are all off painting somewhere this evening. The light in June is so spectacular, isn't it?"

Björn took us into his study. It was crammed floor to ceiling with cabinets full of gleaming minerals, rocks, and crystal-filled geodes. The room sparkled as the western sun came through one of the tall windows. He opened a drawer labelled *Fundy* and began to thumb through his maps.

"Here we go," he said, handing a map to me. "This one is from the Department of Natural Resources and zeroes right in on that area. Now, let me just fish out the other one that may be useful for you."

"This is perfect," I said looking at the topography.

"Ah! Here we are." Björn handed Sophie another map which showed the geological history of the area.

"Are you aware of recent industrial development up that way?" I asked. "I mean right on the coast there?"

"I certainly hope there's not. It's been some time since I've been along that particular road. When I taught the introduction class, I used to take my students up that way every fall. I'd take them to Scots Bay to collect rocks, and over to Caroline Beach to see the monument to the shipwreck—*The Caroline*—that's how that beach got its name. Jasper Creek as I recall is fairly isolated, but it's vital to preserve the natural formations along that coast. It's Triassic basalt, you know— 200 million years old. This was a period of tremendous upheaval resulting in a massive flood of basaltic lava, and the formation of North Mountain and Cape Blomidon."

"So it would make sense that the shoreline would be protected," I said.

"Yes, but as with all things bureaucratic, getting the proper protections in place is complicated. For instance, in one of the coves up that way, but closer to Scots Bay, there is evidence that indigenous people came from far and wide because of the rare deposits of chert, also known as flint. Since it can be worked to form a very strong sharp edge, the resident natives quarried it to make arrowheads and also tools and items for daily living. It's an astounding record going back ten thousand years! Yet anyone can simply walk away with remnants of that ancient tool-making workshop. So there it is, a real treasure trove of ancient history, and its random destruction goes on every day."

Björn's knowledge of this prehistoric world seemed to be both a blessing and a curse for him.

"So you're teaching at the university these days?" Sophie asked.

"Just in the summer and fall. I still travel during the winter months. I like to be in the field—literally."

"Are you still exploring those ancient ruins in the Mesopotamia area?" Sophie asked.

"Not to the extent that we could before the Iraq war—it's much harder now, and, tragically, so much has been looted and destroyed. But one of the field trips I recall vividly involves you. Remember, Sophie, you had that remarkable dream!"

"Very well, Björn." Both their faces lit up at the recollection.

"Okay, you have to tell me," I said. "What dream?"

"When Sophie and I were spending time together, I was over in Iraq with an archeology team from the University of Pennsylvania, and she was here in Nova Scotia, and one night she had a vivid dream which ended up leading my team to a hidden cache of previously undiscovered clay tablets."

"They were concealed at this ancient temple called The Prince's Daughter," Sophie added.

"Exactly right, Sophie. At Nippur," Björn said. "Oh my goodness, that was a long time ago."

"Thank you so much for these maps," I said. "We'll get them back to you soon."

"No rush. Let me know if you need help interpreting anything. You know where I live. Here, I'll give you my card." He handed one to Sophie. "And be very careful. It's easy to

lose your way, or to trip over roots or to fall into a bog. Make
sure you have water with you…and maybe some good rope."

"We'll be careful—don't worry, Björn. Great to see you
again," Sophie said as we stepped out the door.

"What a resource he is!" I said to Sophie as we got into
Old Solid.

"He's just as I remember him, Roz, honestly—do anything
for you. Actually, he's made me feel hopeful. Now, let's go
back to the cottage and suss out our plan for tomorrow."

"First we need to run into Canning and pick up a few
groceries for tonight," I said, turning left onto the main
road.

"Nothing in the fridge, Roz?" she teased.

"You know me, Sophie, I can't seem to get a handle on
the food thing."

"You're worse than McBride."

"No way, he gets the prize. I'm a domestic paragon com-
pared to him."

This got us both giggling, but suddenly Sophie's worst
fears bubbled to the surface.

"Oh, dammit! I hate crying. What's going to happen?"

I motioned to the glove compartment where I kept a box
of tissues.

"It's okay, I'm okay," she said, blowing her nose.

"We're going to find McBride," I said.

"We have to."

"We will," I said, as we drove past the Canning Aboiteau
turn-off.

I was signalling left, waiting to pull into the busy parking
area beside the Canning grocery store, when I spotted the
unforgettable Range Rover nosed in against the building.

My heart jumped into my mouth. "Oh my God."

"What?" Sophie asked looking up. She was engrossed in one of the maps.

"It's them—I'm certain that's the SUV."

Sophie looked at it. "Well then, they must be in the grocery store, right? Let's wait and follow them, Roz. They could lead us to McBride."

"They'll recognize this car, Sophie. It could be dangerous."

"We don't really have a choice, do we?" she said. I looked at her. She was flushed with determination. She wanted this pursuit—this chance at finding McBride.

I switched my signal from left to right and pulled off into an empty lot across the road. My car was now partly concealed by a van parked on the street, and partly by a large wooden *For Sale* sign, but we had a narrow view across the road to the grocery store's glass doors, which were busy with dinnertime customers coming and going.

Then, with a sudden shiver, I recognized one of the men coming out of the store. It was the interrogator, the one who had pushed me into the back seat and put the restraints on my wrists.

But what happened next took my breath away. Following him out the door, carrying the grocery bags, was not his partner, the SUV driver, but someone else.

I looked at Sophie. "What's going on here? That's Jacob!"

Chapter 11

As we watched, the interrogator got in on the passenger's side. Jacob put the supplies in the back and then got behind the wheel, reversed, turned, and drove out of the lot. He entered the main road and made a left at the Boer War Monument, heading up the 358 towards North Mountain.

"I think I'm in shock, Sophie," I said, realizing that Jacob was either a very recent recruit, or he had been working for them all along and had said nothing.

"Come on, Roz. Let's go! Before they get too far ahead."

I started the engine just as my phone bleeped. "It's a Wolfville number," I said glancing at the screen.

"It might be the vet. Better take it," Sophie said.

"You take it." I handed her the phone. "I'll drive, so we don't lose them." I pulled out of the empty lot, and signalled to turn at the monument.

"Yes?" Sophie said. "Constable Cudmore?" She looked at me.

"Oh, God. Just a sec," I said.

"Roz will be with you right away."

I turned the corner and pulled over to the side of the road and took the phone.

"Constable Cudmore, of course, I remember you from yesterday morning. What's up?"

"I'm on assignment from Corporal Monaghan. She sent me up Jasper Creek Road to take a look around. She wanted me to get in touch with you."

"Have you found something?"

"I've found Mr. McBride's car."

"You have? A red Subaru wagon?" I locked eyes with Sophie, and put the phone on speaker.

"It's his. I've checked the plate number," he said.

"Where is it?"

"Uh…there's a quarry along that road—"

"I know where you mean. There's a hand-painted sign across the road from the quarry entrance, right?"

"Yup. It's parked in there."

"But he's not there?"

"No sign of him."

"Anything else catch your eye—any evidence of a scuffle?"

"No, ma'am. Just the car."

"Is it locked?"

"Yes it is. Corporal Monaghan wants me to leave it in place for now, in case Mr. McBride gets back to it."

"In case?" Sophie mouthed to me.

"What else can you tell me, Constable Cudmore? Did you go to the end of the road and check out the bridge?"

"This is as far as I got. I'm off duty now, so I'm heading back to the detachment." I rolled my eyes, remembering how easily he had given up on seeing the girl in the tree.

"Will you be going back out that way sometime soon?"

"It all depends on my orders."

"Please don't hesitate call me if something else comes to light. Even if you think it's nothing. Even if it's the middle of the night."

"Yes, ma'am." He ended the call.

"The last person I expected to hear from," I said to Sophie.

"You see, Roz, you did get things moving this afternoon, and they found Ruby! So let's get going. If we do nothing else tonight, we can at least get a look at McBride's car."

"What about eating? Are you okay, Sophie?" I asked.

She reached down into her bag and pulled out a granola bar. "I've got two of these, an apple, and half a bottle of water. We'll be fine. And we've got the maps."

"Okay. Here we go." I signalled to pull out into the traffic and headed up the 358. The SUV would be well ahead of us by now. There were plenty of cars on the winding road with people heading home, or coming down from the North Mountain communities to attend evening events in the valley. It was almost 7 P.M. but there were still a couple of hours of light. We needed to get to the quarry, and I hoped we would also have enough time to take a good look around.

While I drove, Sophie studied the map. "Oh—there's the quarry. It looks like there's just the one," she said as we turned onto Jasper Creek Road.

"It's down near the end of this road, close to the Bay of Fundy."

"That's right," she said. "It looks tiny on the map. What do they quarry there?"

"I'm assuming it's sand and gravel for construction projects."

"But why would McBride's car be parked there?"

"That's the question, Sophie. Did he park it there? Did someone else stash it there? We don't know."

I slowed down as we passed the driveway to the arts centre to see if there was any sign of Jacob or the SUV, but all was quiet. I had no way of knowing whether Jacob was actually working for the thugs, or if it was under duress. It would explain his reluctance to talk to me, those serious warnings about crossing the bridge, and his knowledge of the guard dogs. But did he have direct knowledge about McBride?

I needed answers and at the moment there were none. We drove along in silence for a couple of kilometres. I glanced at Sophie. She was working hard to keep herself distracted.

"I never even asked you how Toronto was," I said.

"Oh, it was…Toronto. Let's face it, I have a love/hate relationship with that city. But I do have some old friends there who I stayed with—actors I went to the National Theatre School with—so great to see them. I did a couple of decent auditions. One was for a new crime series which I think I might actually get work on."

"That's great news. What would you do, move up there?"

"Oh no. It would only be for two or three months. It's a big production company. My agent thinks they'd take care of accommodations and so on. They hope to start shooting in late August. I should know soon, so fingers crossed. Maybe McBride could even come with me for a stretch—that's what I was thinking, but…." She trailed off. We both felt the fear grab us as the conversation veered back around to the present situation.

"Oh—quarry's coming up!" I said. I slowed down to prepare to turn in. But just then a large tanker truck loomed in the entrance, signalling to pull out. I came to a halt on the narrow shoulder to allow the truck to clear. I fully expected the driver to pull around me and head towards the valley. But instead he turned right, driving towards the Bay of Fundy. We watched the truck disappear over a low rise, its silver tank shining in the early evening sun.

"Now why on earth would he go that way?" I said.

"Well, what's down there?"

"Of course!"

"What?"

"He must be going down there to cross that industrial

bridge! What other reason is there to go that way? I mean, it's the end of the road. Let's follow him and find out."

"No! C'mon, Roz, we have to go in here first and take a look at Ruby Sube. Please! I have to lay eyes on that car." Sophie was distraught. My instincts were to follow the tanker, but I gave in.

"You're right. Let's at least see whether the car is actually there."

The quarry wasn't large. The open section felt about the size of a baseball diamond. There were various piles of different grades of gravel and sand and slate, and impressive piles of sliced rock, which had clearly been quarried directly out of a high outcropping that formed the back end of the area.

There she was. Ruby Sube! Tucked in close to the trees on our left. More central, and near the back of the quarry, was a rickety camper-trailer that possibly served as an office, but for the time being we had the place to ourselves. I drove over and parked next to Ruby, nosing in towards the trees and undergrowth that grew along either side of the quarry. Sophie and I got out. I couldn't see anything of particular interest on the ground around McBride's car. Sophie bent down and tried to peer in through the windows on the passenger's side.

I stood by the driver's door and smiled at her across the roof. "I have a key," I said.

"Handy." She smiled back.

I'd picked McBride's car up on many occasions while I was working for him and still carried the key on my ring. I opened the door, got in, and reached across to unlock the passenger's side for Sophie. The two of us sat silently in the glow of the low sun, staring into the trees, trying desperately to imagine what could have befallen McBride and where he was now. There didn't seem to be any clues in the car—though the floor of the back seat was its usual collection of papers, plastic bags, fast food wrappers, and crumpled coffee cups.

"Not the tidiest," I said drily.

"He's working on it," Sophie said, "but honestly, Roz, the house was a sight!"

"Oh, dear. If he'd made it home, I know he would have cleaned it up for you. Listen, since we're here, I'm going to quickly scout the circumference of the quarry and see what there is to see."

"I just need to sit here for a minute," she said.

I jogged up to the rear boundary of the quarry and behind the old trailer, which had a couple of small windows that were held together with masking tape and covered on the inside by old bent venetian blinds. I paused and stared. Could he be in there?

I ran around to the front of the trailer and up some little steps. I knocked. Then I tried the door, but it was locked. If I stood on my toes, I could see most of the area inside through the filthy door-window. There was a cluttered desk and an old swivel chair with ripped upholstery, a sink and cupboard area, and a narrow cot. That was it.

I resumed my circuitous inspection of the quarry borders. The rock face along the back was fairly high and sheer and extended across the entire width of the quarry. Then I turned to explore the side opposite to where we had parked. Alders and other undergrowth formed the border. Assorted grades of gravel extended in piles from the back all the way to the ditch by the road. As I made my way along the edge between the gravel and the bush, something on the ground just beyond the boundary caught my eye. I moved in among the trees to get a closer look. Unmistakable.

I picked it up, legged it back across the quarry, and slid into the driver's seat beside Sophie. "Look what I found!" I handed her Molly's round white water dish.

"Oh, Roz."

"So McBride has been here with Molly! He must have let her out of the car for a little exercise and a drink. But did he just forget the water dish—or did something distract him? Was this before he was at the bridge or after?"

We looked at each other. "Who knows?" she said, starting to tear up again.

"Okay listen, Sophie, let's get into my car and go down to the end of the road, to see what we can discover."

Just as we reached for the door handles to let ourselves out, headlights appeared at the entrance and a large tanker truck rumbled into the quarry. Even though it was the back end of McBride's car that faced into the circle, Sophie and I both instinctively slid down in our seats.

The driver carefully maneuvered the truck around so that it was pointing out towards the road and away from us. He jumped down from the cab. On his head was a well-worn Stetson Western.

"Nice hat," Sophie said.

"Check out those kickers!"

"Ancient eh? They've seen a lot of miles."

I watched him in my side mirror as he walked to his left and behind a small mountain of quarried gravel.

"Now what's he doing?" I muttered.

"Nature calls?" Sophie ventured. "So, is that the same truck we just saw coming back now, or what?"

"No. It's the same style of tank but the cab is different, and this one approached from the valley, not the Bay of Fundy. You know what? A tanker truck almost forced me off this road last night. What are all these tankers doing? I mean, they're certainly not here to pick up gravel."

"What do you think is in those shiny silver tanks?" Sophie asked.

"Thousands of gallons of something…."

"There he is," Sophie said, peeking between our two seats and out through the rear window of Ruby Sube.

We watched him as he took his phone out of his denim shirt pocket, punched in some numbers, and paced around in front of his truck. He spoke, then nodded his head and looked at his watch. He put his phone away, leaned back against the front grill, took out a package of cigarettes, and lit one.

"Players," I said.

"Central casting," added Sophie.

"It's a waiting game. What's he waiting for?"

"Maybe he's waiting for that other one."

"Like for a meeting, or…no—that's it! You've got it, Sophie!"

"What have I got?"

"There must be room for only one tanker at a time! That's why they come in here—they're using this quarry as a kind of holding pen while they wait."

As if on cue, the tanker we had seen when we first arrived rumbled by the quarry entrance, making its way back along Jasper Creek Road towards the valley. It gave a short blast of its horn as it passed the entrance. Our driver, still leaning against his truck, dropped his cigarette, ground it out, and pushed himself away from the grill. He ambled around to the driver's side and climbed up into the cab. He started up the engine and the tanker lumbered forward to the entrance, and pulled out, heading right, towards Fundy.

After a couple of minutes, we got into Old Solid and followed him. The sun was a red ball low in the sky.

"I was here at exactly the same time last night," I said. "Oh, and I was here this morning too. No wonder I feel like I'm getting nowhere."

"That's not true, Roz," Sophie said. "If you hadn't been here this morning, you wouldn't have found Molly. And you had no choice but to get her out of here and straight to the vet."

"You're right," I said. "But why oh why haven't we heard anything from McBride?"

We were passing the dirt lane that went off to the left behind the cabins.

"You know what? I'm going to pull in here and ditch the car," I said to Sophie. "In case Jacob and our friend in the SUV happen by and recognize Old Solid."

I turned left and drove along behind the camps. Each property had a little driveway. I chose the third one and tucked my car in between what looked like a well house and the cabin. There was no sign of any summer-dwellers. The windows had their protective shutters in place. "Winter and July," I said.

"Okay, here we go." We jumped out. I grabbed my grey hoodie from the back seat, and Sophie put on her leather jacket. She tucked the folded maps into her bag and slung it over her shoulder. I locked the car and we walked rapidly out to Jasper Creek Road. The light was a kind of pre-dusk purple and it was getting chilly. I pulled on my hoodie. The air was sweet with the unmistakable smell of brine.

We could hear the roar of a truck engine and, looking beyond the bridge, we caught sight of the tanker disappearing into the spruce forest at the top of the high promontory overlooking the bay.

"That's gotta be our cowboy!" Sophie said.

"Yeehaw!" I said, smiling. "This means the quarry, the tankers, and the bridge are all connected! McBride must have been piecing it all together when they got him. There must be a building up there or a depot or…."

"So back to the question: how do we get up there?" Sophie said, champing at the bit.

"That's what I meant about crossing the creek further inland and making our way through the undergrowth to the top of ridge."

"So we really can't just go straight up there from here?" There was an impatient edge in her voice.

"As much as I'd love to do that right now and see what's going on with that rig, we'd be jumping the gun, especially if there are guard dogs up there. And we know Molly was attacked, Sophie—those dogs are real."

"Then let's go with your plan, Roz. Come back early tomorrow and find that creek further inland, and make our way to the top." She patted her bag. "We've got the maps."

"Great," I said. "That's what we'll do."

We started to head back to my car. We'd just turned onto the lane behind the cabins when headlights coming along Jasper Creek Road lit up the trees on our right. I caught a quick glimpse of a blue pickup.

"You look," I said to Sophie, keeping myself turned away from the lights. The vehicle sped past the lane and continued towards the slope that led down to the wharf. "What was it?" I said.

"A small truck. I think it's blue—it's a bit too dark to know for sure."

"Was it a Ford?" I asked.

"Could be." I always teased Sophie because she could never tell one make of vehicle from another.

"It's gotta be buddy from this morning who called me a gawker and told me to mind my own business."

"Go get your car, Roz. I'm just going to whip back along the side of the road and take a peek down to see what he's up to. Don't worry—if he questions me I'll tell him I lost my hat or something. I mean, it's still a public beach. I'll meet you right back here at this turnoff."

Before I could stop her she had darted back out onto Jasper Creek Road and was running towards the top of the slope. I picked up my pace. I didn't want Sophie out there in the dark in the same place where I'd recently lost McBride.

∞

My fears were unfounded. Sophie was right where she said she'd be and jumped in beside me, just as the sun sank below the horizon.

"So who is he and what's he doing?" I asked.

"It *is* an older fella, with a plaid jacket and a peaked cap."

"That's him," I said. "Mind you, that description fits most of the old boys in the Valley."

"And most of the young ones." Sophie grinned.

"So what's he doing?" I asked her.

"He's over by the bridge, right where the cable connects to the steel pole. He's got a little wooden crate down there to sit on. Looks like he's just waiting."

"So maybe he's manning the cable," I said. "Where's his truck?"

"Down in the parking area, by those sheds."

"Yup. That's exactly where it was parked earlier. Well, it's good that you checked him out, Sophie. He must be on the payroll. That would account for his push-me-away attitude this morning."

"I just wanted to make sure he didn't have McBride with him," she said.

"No stone unturned," I said. We pulled onto Jasper Creek Road and began driving back towards the valley. I glanced at her. "We're going to find him."

A few minutes later, we passed the entrance to the quarry on our left and I slowed down so that we could get a good look in as we went by. Sure enough, another tanker truck was parked there, waiting, its nose pointed out towards the road. Waiting for our cowboy to drive by and signal that the coast was clear, that now it was this one's turn to cross the Jasper Creek bridge.

Chapter 12

WHEN WE ARRIVED BACK AT the cottage, Sophie and I were stressed, exhausted, and hungry, and we still hadn't made it to the grocery store.

"Guess what? I have a can of chicken noodle soup," I said.

"That's pathetic, Roz. But it sounds delicious—heat it up immediately!"

"You heat it up and I'll make a fire. After we eat, let's take a close look at those maps."

We sat in the living room by the stove and ate soup while munching down the half package of saltines I had brought along from the city. The cat ate her dinner too, and stretched out on the mat in front of the fire.

"This is a great place to stay," Sophie said, finally relaxing a little. "You're planning to work on the Beckett here, right?"

"Yes, and the Beckett gang actually paid me a surprise visit. They sort of arrived in the middle of everything and after McBride left, we had a meeting about the project. I'm still hoping to work with them next week up at that arts centre. Sophie, remember when we did Beckett's *Happy Days*, and you played Winnie?"

"How could I forget—buried to the waist in that papier-mâché mound. 'Another happy day.' That's how we got to know each other, Roz, madly figuring it all out."

"I can still see you holding the parasol," I said.

"That spontaneously combusts on cue! Talk about a technical nightmare!"

"And then in the second act, buried up to your neck."

"I'd love to be working with you guys on the short works. I've always wanted to play that woman in Beckett's *Eh Joe*—do you know it?"

I stopped still.

Sophie went on. "I learned it once for a workshop. It's actually a voice-over—you don't see her. She's the voice in his head—"

I could feel my blood run cold.

"—Roz? Are you all right?"

"Sophie, now that you say it…it's…."

"What?"

"That's what she reminded me of. That's the image that's been just under the surface, that's been haunting me."

"Who? She?"

"When I saw the girl out there in the basin, before she was tied to the frame and lifted into the helicopter, she was placed on the sandbar, facing out across the water, and it was like she was staring at me.

"There's that section in *Eh Joe*, I think it's right near the end. She's taken the pills and she lies down a few feet from the tide…do you remember from the script, the description of her eyes…?"

"Right, right, give me a second…" Sophie said, and then: "'pale…the pale eyes…The way they opened after….'"

"Yes—that's the line! It reminds me of her."

"Really—that whole piece is eerie," Sophie said, "…the lavender slip, the gillette…."

"You know what, Sophie? I'm fairly certain she stayed right here in this cottage in late April, early May."

"Who, you mean the dead girl?"

"Yes. Aurelia Strange. That's her name. I think she and the girl in the tree are the same person."

"But Roz, I mean April's almost two months. How do you know her name, anyway?"

I told Sophie about Ellie finding the journal in the loft the day before, and what I'd learned from the newspaper clipping about her. "Also, there was a receipt tucked in the notebook so while I was waiting for your bus I went into the shop in Wolfville where it was purchased and the clerk remembered that the girl who bought the journal had red hair and pale skin—just like the girl in the tree!" Breathless, I pointed towards the basin.

Sophie shook her head. "There are lots of women with red hair, especially around here."

"But this girl, Aurelia Strange, was a young award-winning journalist, and according to the only entry she made in that little notebook, she was moving to a cabin up on the Bay of Fundy to be closer to 'the daily activity'—something she was investigating—and she was planning to do an interview that could be 'treacherous.' It all fits, right? I mean, someone tied her into that tree! That sounds treacherous to me."

"But you have no proof that the girl whose body was recovered by the helicopter is this journalist. And until her identity is published, you won't know."

"And now that this case is 'classified' and in the hands of the so-called 'higher-ups,' that information may never be forthcoming. Do you want to see the pictures of her?"

"Of course I do. Show me."

I got out my phone and we pored over the images. We came to the image of the girl lying on the sandbar after being disentangled from the roots, her arms out in front of her, one crossed over the other. She was on her right side, facing out towards the basin just as I remembered.

"But her eyes are closed," Sophie said, looking at me.

"I know. That's so strange—honestly, when I took the photo, I swear she was looking right at me."

"Sometimes we see what we want to see, and you wanted her to be alive," Sophie said, leaning in to study the photo. "I think there's a ring on her finger. Can you zoom in and make her hand clearer?"

I brought the girl's left hand into full view.

"It's a signet ring for something," Sophie said.

"That's King's, Sophie. It's a King's College ring! There you go. The newspaper article said Aurelia Strange graduated with honours from the journalism school at King's in 2012!"

I started pacing around the living room. "This is crazy," I said. "I need to tell someone who I think she is."

"Don't get distracted, Roz. We have to stay focused on finding McBride. We have to stick with tomorrow's plan."

I looked at Sophie, and could see she was panicking at the thought that finding her husband might have become secondary.

"No, you're right. We'd better prepare for that hike," I said, reassuring her.

"Okay, good. I'll get out the maps."

"And I will recharge this phone," I said, taking it into the living room.

"Wow, this coast—this Fundy coastline!" Sophie said, spreading out Björn's maps on the big table in the porch. "There are so many falls and coves—and what are these things called 'vaults'?"

"They sound like places where pirates stash gold, don't they? And there is plenty of lore about hidden treasure all along that coast. But I think I've read that vaults are deep holes that have formed naturally. So, sometimes, treasure did get hidden in them."

We sat and studied the map of Jasper Creek Road and surrounds, and concluded that we'd best start our hike on a cart track which looked to be right behind the quarry. That would lead us directly to the brook. However, once on the other side of the brook, the track turned and went inland, away from the coast. "So, after we cross, we would need to follow the brook towards the coast," I said.

"But before we get near the new bridge, we need to judge when to move away from the brook and start our covert climb up to the top of the bluff," Sophie said.

"Right. Hopefully it won't be too boggy or overgrown. It's a long way up."

"Björn's map makes it look straightforward. In fact, you know what, Roz? This could be exactly what McBride did. He said he was by the bridge when he was talking to you, but when he realized he couldn't cross it without being stopped, he may have decided to get up to the top another way. That could be why his car is parked in the quarry. And we know Molly was with him at that point. So whatever happened to him, or to Molly, could have happened on the way up there."

"Right. We need to be prepared for anything," I said.

Sophie stood up and stretched. "Man, I'm really exhausted."

"Get some sleep. I'll see you in the morning."

She abruptly put her hands on my shoulders, and spoke: "Let's make a pledge, Roz. We're going to find him!"

I reached out and put my hands on her shoulders, and we looked at one another. Together we said, "We're going to find him!"

"Good night, Sophie," I said.

Sophie had selected the middle bedroom off the living room. She closed her door. I stayed in the porch thinking about what we would need to take along for our trek, and then

I gathered the bowls from the living room and tidied up the kitchen. I fed the cat, who was a bottomless pit. Good thing I had brought more food along for her than I had for myself.

I stepped out on the stoop for a moment to get some air and thought about the bridge, and the tanker trucks we had seen. I went back inside to look them up.

A few minutes of online research turned up all manner of tankers, the size they come in, what liquids they're able to carry, and how the pumps work. The ones we'd seen crossing the Jasper Creek bridge were the biggies. After about half an hour I decided it was time to pack it in and head to bed. We had a big hike ahead of us in the morning.

I was awakened from a dead sleep by the sound of Sophie's voice. I bolted up, trying to get my bearings in the pitch dark. My feet found the floor. Sophie was crying out loudly, "I can see you! We're coming! Don't, no, please don't slip away." Then I heard her sobbing. I made my way towards her room. There was a night light on in the living room and as I opened her door, I could see her silhouetted in the bed. She was sitting up and reaching out.

"Sophie! Sophie. It's okay. It's me, Roz. Wake up! You're having a dream."

Her eyes opened wide and she stared at me.

"Take it easy," I said. "I'm going to turn your light on, okay?"

"Okay." She was breathing in short gasps.

I found the reading lamp by her bed and clicked it on.

"Oh, Roz…it's McBride. It's very dark where he is. He needs help—he's dying." She abruptly grabbed my wrists. "This was real—I really saw him."

"Sophie, we're going tomorrow to look for him, remember? It's okay. Do you want some water?"

"He kept saying this name—this woman's name."

"What was it?"

"Caroline. He was saying, 'Find Caroline, find Caroline.'"

"Who's Caroline? Why is that ringing a bell? Wait!... Wait just a minute." I hurried out into the porch and turned on the light.

Our map of the Jasper Creek area was still spread out on the table. In tiny letters along the Fundy coastline, just a few short coves down from Jasper Creek, there it was.

I heard Sophie's bare feet padding across the living room into the porch.

"Look, Sophie, you must have seen this when you were studying this map tonight. Right here, just a few coves over from Jasper Creek is Caroline Beach."

"Let me see," she said leaning over the map. "Caroline! That could be it, Roz. Let's go...we need to go there. Now."

"Sophie, listen, it's only 3. It won't be light for another couple of hours. It would be too dangerous."

"Dangerous or not, there's no time to lose."

"We'll go at first light. Let's calm down and have some tea."

I went into the kitchen and put the kettle on. I took a deep breath and tried to think. There were other times Sophie had astonished me with her dreams and premonitions—enough times that I knew her witchy sense was nothing to scoff at. Our scheme to find our way to the top of the bluff where the tankers went wasn't necessarily going to lead us to McBride. And Caroline Beach was only a short distance from Jasper Creek Road. If we found nothing there, we could just carry on with the original plan. Besides, I knew she wouldn't rest until we'd followed up on the dream. The kettle whistled and I poured the water into the pot. Then I heard her voice. Apparently, there was no stopping her.

"Hi, Björn. It's Sophie, I'm so sorry to wake you in the middle of the night, but this is urgent…. No, no, we're okay, it's a long story, but the reason I'm calling is, well, there's something we didn't tell you when we visited you earlier. My husband has gone missing and I think he's trapped somewhere at Caroline Beach up on the Bay of Fundy…. Yes, we did. Roz talked to the RCMP because they found his car up that way, but they're not doing anything more at this point. Oh, and she found his dog on the Fundy shore, very badly injured. The dog's at the vet's now. But, do you know where I mean?… That's right, you mentioned taking your students there. I'm looking at a map. It's not that far from Jasper Creek Road…. Yes, a few coves further along. And are there caves there at Caroline?… You will?… Okay…okay, at dawn…. Around five thirty. The tide? Just a second, I'll ask Roz. Roz? Do you know—"

"I think high tide's going to be around 9:30 this morning," I called from the kitchen.

"Björn? Roz thinks 9:30…. Okay, five then! See you at five. Thank you, Björn. Again, my apologies to you and Grace for calling at this crazy hour. See you soon. We'll be ready."

A moment later, Sophie came into the kitchen. She was crying.

"Oh God, what's wrong?" I said. "You just made something great happen, Sophie."

"I'm so afraid we'll be too late…I mean, I know we have to wait. I'm just so worried."

"I'm worried too, but we'll be there soon. Is Björn going to drive us out there?"

"Yes. He said he has some old drawings and charts he can dig out."

"Drink this tea," I said handing her a cup. "I'm going to make us some oatmeal. That'll set us up for Caroline Beach."

Chapter 13

THE ORANGE GLOW OF THE sun just peeking over the horizon found Sophie and me standing outside the cottage by Longspell Road. When Björn pulled up in his dark green Volvo, Sophie was raring to go. She jumped into the front seat beside him as I climbed into the back.

"Are you all right, Sophie?" was the first thing he said.

"I confess I'm wound up, but I'm very grateful to you, Björn," Sophie replied. "I'll be better once we're on Caroline Beach."

"Which will be very soon," Björn said. "One thing about the early hour is that there's little traffic to contend with. Now Sophie, tell me please why you think your husband is out there?"

Sophie looked back at me. I nodded. It seemed only fair under the circumstances to bring Björn into the picture.

"McBride. That's his name. He's a private investigator," she began. "And Roz often works with him on cases."

"That's right," I said, jumping in. "McBride thought something strange was going on down at the end of Jasper Creek Road."

"What do you mean?" Björn asked, clearly intrigued.

"Well," I continued, "there's a big, shiny industrial-style bridge down there which is apparently off-limits to the public, and has video surveillance."

"That's perplexing," Björn said. "I don't recall ever hearing anything about it."

I explained to Björn what had happened over the last few days in detail, right up to the previous afternoon, when the Mounties found McBride's car at the quarry.

"While we were there we discovered that tanker trucks were waiting in that same quarry, then crossing that bridge and climbing up to the top of the bluff," I added. "We don't know what their purpose is, but we think McBride was onto something."

"That's why we needed your maps," Sophie continued. "To find another way up to the top of the bluff, without crossing the bridge…."

"Which was our plan for today, except that"—I looked at Sophie—"in the middle of the night, Sophie had a vivid dream about McBride in distress at Caroline Beach."

"And, as we know, Sophie has very prescient dreams. This really doesn't surprise me," Björn said, glancing over at her with a little grin.

"Are you teasing me, Björn?" Sophie asked.

"On the contrary! Why do you think I'm here, driving you around at 5 a.m.? I'm a believer!"

Once on Gospel Woods Road, we drove past the turnoff to Jasper Creek Road and took the next right turn, which Björn said would land us much closer to Caroline Beach. After several kilometres, we turned onto a single-lane dirt track for the final leg. When we reached the Fundy shore, we parked the car under the trees and began to pick our way down through the rocks and onto the beach. Björn carried a backpack containing useful things like rope, a flashlight, water, and some tools. He was in his element. Once we were all walking freely along the shore, he took a deep breath.

"What a morning! Look at the early sun lighting up Cape Split!" he said, pointing across the water.

"We never could have found our way here without you," I said.

"Yes, that little back road is a well-kept secret. And at high tide this coast is treacherous, but luckily we have some time. Now—two short coves along here to the west is Caroline Beach. You'll know we're there because you'll see the blue marble monument I told you about that looks like a gravestone. The *Caroline* ran aground here in December of 1831, five frozen bodies on board and all the other passengers and crew missing. A mystery and a tragedy.

"There are numerous sea caves along the shore, as I recall. Certainly big enough for a man to walk into, but some of them are swamped when the tide is high. So we are here early enough to take a good look."

We arrived at the second cove, which formed a wide curve around the area known as Caroline Beach. We paused at the monument. I looked along the jagged shoreline. In the centre of the cove was a point where two huge rock faces came together in a kind of V. Right at the point's vortex was a dark jagged cut, not so much a cave opening as a narrow crevice.

"Is that an actual opening into the rock?" I asked Björn.

"It is," he said. "As I recall, there's a smooth floor beyond it and then it drops down a little, and then further in, there is another steep drop—almost like a well."

Sophie's hand was over her mouth. "I—this is what I saw, Roz. I think this is it!" she said, nodding at Björn. She broke into a run. I was right behind her.

Just as we arrived at the opening, we were startled to see someone backing out of the crevice onto the beach. As we stood catching our breath and silently watching, the person freed himself from the fissure and stood fully up. He was facing the rock. Then he turned and saw me. It was Jacob. A look of disbelief and shock was in his eyes. He tore off along the beach to the west.

I dropped my bag and ran after him. "Stop—Jacob! Please." I picked up my pace, managed to grab onto his jacket, and then tackled him just as he was about to clamber up onto a path through the underbrush.

"Ow! Jesus," he said, as we both landed hard on the gravel shore.

"What are you doing here? What's going on?" I said, pushing down on his shoulders and holding him to the ground.

"It's a public beach! Leave me alone—get off me!"

"No. I need answers, Jacob. You've been lying to me."

"I just…I brought him some water…but he's…."

"What? He's what? Dead?"

"No…no, no—he's—I think he's unconscious, dehydrated. He's breathing. I took the gag from his mouth. He swallowed a little water, but he's not—his eyes didn't open."

"Okay. So McBride's in there!" I said, almost tearing up. I looked back toward the cave opening; Sophie and Björn were not in sight. They must have found McBride by now. "How did you know he was here?" I said, gripping Jacob's shoulders.

"After you told me about finding his dog on the beach yesterday—I just thought he might be…I decided to come and check out the caves this morning at low tide. I came to help him. But…what are you doing here? How did you know where to look?"

"We're searching, Jacob—that's what we're doing. We've been looking for McBride for two days! You knew I was looking for him and you didn't say anything. So fill me in. Did they drag his body across the beach? How did it work?"

"I wasn't there. I didn't even know he was in there. I just guessed that he might be. And I was right."

"So when you found him, why didn't you report it?"

"I just found him now—this morning. I was going to report it."

"Then why did you run when you saw me?"

Jacob didn't answer. He awkwardly turned his head, looking out at the Bay of Fundy.

"Talk to me, or I'll have the cops on you."

"Didn't I tell you yesterday to report him missing—remember? Why would I do that if I didn't want to help you find him?"

"Well, now there will be a police report on McBride and you're going to be part of that report, Jacob. You do realize your involvement in all this is serious."

"I'm not an idiot."

"No, you're not. In fact, I think you're really smart and a good person. But maybe those thugs with their fancy armoured SUV make you feel important."

"What thugs? I don't have a clue what you're talking about."

"Look, cut the crap! I saw you leaving the grocery store last night carrying their supplies, playing chauffeur."

"It's just the occasional errand. It's a job, that's all. It's nothing."

"You're way out of your depth with those guys, Jacob. Come clean and tell me what you know. You can call it a job, but by the time you decide you've had enough, it might be too late."

At that moment my attention was pulled back to the cleft in the rock, where I saw Björn push his way out into the light and hurriedly get on his cell phone.

"Oh dear, what's happening?" I said, watching him. He finished the call, looked along the beach until he saw me, and began walking quickly towards us. I was still sitting on top of Jacob, holding him down.

"How is he?" I called out to Björn.

"He's alive, Roz."

"Thank God for that."

"I just called the ambulance. Probably twenty minutes. It comes from Kentville. I think we got here just in time. Sophie is with him. Are you all right?" Björn asked as he got closer to us.

"I'm a little bruised, I think. This is Jacob. This is Björn." Jacob turned his head awkwardly and nodded.

"Hello," Björn said, somewhat perplexed. He looked at me. "So you two know each other?"

"We're acquainted." I put my hands on Jacob's shoulders and pushed myself up to a standing position. "Jacob's the one I mentioned earlier who warned me about the guard dogs. He says he was just here bringing some water to McBride."

I stepped away from Jacob and looked back at him. "We're not done, you and I, but right now I'm going to see McBride."

"I'm going back to the car, Roz," Björn said. "I'll drive out to the road proper, to wait for the ambulance and lead the medics in."

"I'll come with you," Jacob said to Björn.

I ran back along the beach to the fissure in the rock, picked my bag up from where I'd dropped it, and stepped carefully through the crevice into the darkness. I stood still for a moment, waiting for my eyes to adjust.

"Roz," Sophie said. "We're just over here."

As I moved further in towards her voice, my shadow cleared the entrance and the light coming through brightened the space.

"Oh, Sophie," I said, seeing McBride lying on the ground. Sophie had folded her shawl and placed it under his head. I bent down beside them. "Is he awake?"

"He's in and out. When we cut the restraints from his wrists and ankles, he came around for a minute. He knows I'm here. I can feel his heart beating."

She took my hand and put it on McBride's heart. "It feels strong, doesn't it?" she said.

"McBride's pretty tough."

"I hope so…."

"Sophie, you're amazing. You saved his life! You found him."

"He's the man of my dreams, Roz. Literally," she said, laughing and crying.

I looked around the interior of the cavern. The floor was gravel, rocks, sand, and bits of shells and seaweed. By the sidewall, a few feet beyond McBride, something shiny glinted and caught my eye. "What is that?" I said. Standing to my full height was just possible in the centre area, and as I moved towards the side I had to stoop over. I reached the point where the floor met the sidewall, and crouched down. What had caught my eye was a silver lipstick tube.

I went to pick it up and examine it, but my training kicked in and I realized I shouldn't touch it. The top was missing, and the lipstick itself was almost gone, roughly worn away. I looked at the rock face that rose up near it, but it was too murky to see clearly.

"Do you have a flashlight, Sophie?" I said.

"There's a small one on my key chain," she said, reaching into her jacket pocket.

"Perfect." I shone the light over the rock face. It was low to the ground I spotted the letters, awkwardly drawn with the cherry-coloured lipstick: *A-U-R-E-L* and then nothing.

"Sophie. She was here. This must be where they kept her before they—"

"Kept who?"

"Aurelia…. She's written the first letters of her name here. This proves they're one and the same—Aurelia and the girl in the tree. Doesn't it?"

"I don't know, Roz—I…it's all so crazy."

I quickly took a picture of the scrawled letters with my phone, and then found a baggie in my rucksack and used it to pick up the lipstick tube. I returned the key chain to Sophie, and asked her to shine her flashlight on McBride so I could get a picture of him on the floor of the cave. McBride's eyelids fluttered open, and he mumbled something.

"What did you say?" Sophie asked leaning over. He whispered in her ear. She looked up at me smiling. "He says he's ready for his close-up."

Chapter 14

THE SHRIEK OF THE AMBULANCE broke the early morning silence. Sophie and I looked at one another, relieved.

I leaned over and put my hand on McBride's shoulder. "Help has arrived, my friend."

I ducked out through the opening and into the light. I was startled by how far the tide had advanced. I paced around in a state of unease, thinking about Aurelia and the startling evidence I had just found on the cave wall.

Finally, the paramedics appeared, a man and a woman, rounding the bend in the shoreline, running with their medical gear and a stretcher. Björn led them.

"Roz, this is Charlene and J. P.," he said indicating the medics.

"You two are heroes," I said.

"Heroes or fools," Charlene said, looking at her partner.

"We're breaking all the rules today," J. P. said as he shoved his gear through the opening.

They maneuvered themselves and the stretcher awkwardly through the crevice in the rock. I could see that getting it back out of the cave with McBride strapped to it wasn't going to be easy .

"What did they mean about the rules?" I asked Björn.

"Once the tide is this far in, they're supposed to have water rescue in place just in case. And I don't think that dirt track up there is actually a road. But I convinced them they'd be able to turn the ambulance around—which they have already done."

"You're the real hero," I said to Björn. "Jacob ran off, I suppose."

"Not exactly. He asked me to tell you he had to go to work at the arts centre. He says he lives close by—just above the beach here on Old Mill Road. So he went home to get his car."

"That's right. When McBride and I first met him, I remember him telling us he lived out this way with his mother and sister."

"You know, I like him," Björn said. "But what's his involvement in all this?"

"I'm not sure, but he knows a lot more than he's telling me. And whoever did this to McBride isn't who he should be hanging around with, much less working for."

Sophie emerged. "Okay," she said. "They've got him secured. Here we go."

The medics rolled the stretcher very carefully out of the cave at ground level, and then lifted it. McBride was grimy with blood and dirt, his face badly bruised, his lip swollen, and he could not stay fully conscious for long. It took the three of us to keep the way cleared of rocks and bits of driftwood as they rapidly negotiated a path from the cave to the ambulance.

When we finally got him up onto the road, Sophie asked if she could ride along, and they told her they'd be breaking another rule.

"Oh well, in for a penny.... Go on, get in," Charlene said.

As I had observed over the years, if Sophie wanted something, people somehow couldn't say no. I hugged her, and she climbed up into the ambulance. Björn and I watched as it sped off with the siren blaring.

My plan was to return with Björn to Kingsport, where I would get my car and then join them at the Kentville hospital. We drove in silence for a few minutes. Then he spoke:

"What are you going to do about this, Roz? There's been a crime. This was a serious assault on McBride. He may have been left there to die. And he likely would have died if we hadn't found him by some crazy Sophie miracle. That's twice she's astounded me with her dreams."

"There are more things, Horatio," I said, as we turned left onto Gospel Woods Road and began to make our way towards the valley turn-off.

"When are you going to contact the police?" he asked.

"You're right. There is a crime, and I think this business with McBride is just a small part of something much larger. When I asked the police to help me look for him yesterday, they certainly didn't jump in with both feet, though later they did send out a constable who managed to find his car. But then he went off duty and they didn't take it any further. On the other hand, they had warned McBride—and me—to keep our noses out of what we had begun to investigate. In my experience that either means there's a cover-up, or the police are in the midst of their own investigation and don't want us to stir the pot."

"But you think what happened to McBride is connected to the industrial bridge and the trucks you mentioned earlier."

"Everything points that way. That's what McBride was investigating when he disappeared. Once he's conscious and hopefully able to tell us exactly what went down, we'll arrive at a course of action. Don't worry, Björn, we won't just walk away from this."

"And what about right now, Roz?" He pointed in the direction of Jasper Creek Road. "Should we take a quick run down there?"

"You want to see that bridge for yourself, don't you?"

"North Mountain is part of my world—I need to see what they're doing to it!"

"Let me call Sophie first, just to check in."

He pulled over to the side just before the turn-off to Jasper Creek Road.

"Sophie! How are things going?... He did? That's two jokes!... Listen, Björn and I were just thinking of taking a quick run down Jasper Creek Road. I could pick up McBride's car at the quarry and then we'll have it, but I wanted to make sure you were okay first.... I'll see you soon. Don't hesitate to call if need be." I could feel myself relax a little as I put the phone away. "They're getting ready to check him in. She sounds relieved."

"So...?" Björn asked.

"So yes, let's go!" Björn pulled away from the side of the road and turned left, heading down the now familiar Jasper Creek Road to the coast.

"Open the glove compartment, Roz," he directed me. "There's some trail mix in there—I'm a little bit hungry. And there's a bottle of water in the door there if you're thirsty."

"Perfect," I said.

After a couple of kilometres, we were about to pass the driveway to the arts centre. "Do you know this place?" Björn asked. "Grace and I enjoy coming up here in the summer to see their performances—always wonderful plays, interesting actors. And all off the grid!"

"How long have you and Grace lived in the Valley?"

"We bought that house in Kingsport seven years ago, when I took the job at the university. I already knew the area quite well from my years of researching the Fundy shoreline. Grace and I had spent time vacationing up here, and when that Kingsport house came up for sale we jumped at it."

"I don't blame you—it's a fabulous place. It's a big house."

"Well, Grace has a large studio on the second floor. She's a well-known painter. She has an agent in Ontario—she used to work in Toronto. But now, you couldn't pry her out of Nova Scotia."

"You mentioned that she was out painting with a water-colour group. I didn't realize she was a professional artist."

"She started the group—loves it—they find all kinds of interesting places to paint, and she says there are several inspired painters among them. What about you, Roz? You said you work with Mr. McBride?"

"I did for several years, but right now I have a research job with the Prosecution Service. I'm a criminologist. But I also work in the theatre. That's how Sophie and I first met. I was planning to spend this vacation investigating Samuel Beckett's short plays. It's a project I've begun working on with a company of four actors."

"I'm very fond of Samuel Beckett," Björn said.

"Really, Björn! Are you joking?"

"I'm quite serious. I grew up seeing some of his work in Denmark. He was very popular—you know we Danes like the dark stuff. It's those long winters."

"Oh! There's the sign coming up—do you see it? The quarry entrance is just across the road from it."

From what I could see of the quarry, all was quiet. McBride's car was still sitting on the far side, barely visible through the tall roadside trees and brush.

"So let's take a look at the bridge first, and on the way back I'll pick up his car and go straight to the hospital from here. That is, unless there's a great big tanker truck blocking the entrance."

I explained to Björn how Sophie and I had concluded the

quarry was used as a holding area if there was more than one tanker truck waiting to cross the bridge.

"So do you have any theories about what they're actually doing?"

"That's the question, isn't it."

"How large are they?"

"I looked them up online last night. They're the biggies—single tanks. It said they carry eight to ten thousand gallons."

Björn raised his eyebrows. "Serious business then."

We were almost at the end of the road. As we approached the top of the slope, he abruptly braked and came to a stop. "Look there!" he said.

A tanker truck was descending from the high bluff. We watched as the driver negotiated his way to the bottom of the hill, and then proceeded onto the bridge. Standing by the left-hand post, the old codger released the cable for him.

"This is good timing!" I said. "You get to see for yourself what I'm talking about."

"That bridge is a major installation, Roz—and what on earth was that tanker doing up there?"

The truck began rumbling up towards us. Björn hastily pulled his Volvo as far onto the right shoulder as he could. He opened his door and started to get out.

"Björn! What are you doing?" I called.

"I want to talk to him—find out what's going on." He stepped to the front of his Volvo and gestured to the driver, but the truck roared by him and much too close for comfort. Björn got back into the driver's seat. He smiled at me. "No interest in stopping."

"Nope. I'm relieved he didn't drive right over you."

"I should go down there to the bridge and ask that older fellow what that tanker was doing up there," Björn said.

"That *older fellow* is the one who told me the other morning to mind my own business. I'm sure you'll get the same response. Sophie and I may still try to find a way up there to see what's what. So at this point, I don't want to draw attention to myself. I'm sure he hasn't figured out I'm here with you, but I'd rather not give him that opportunity."

"You're right. And Roz, you should get to the hospital—so, another time!" Björn turned the Volvo around. "Well, now that I've seen it," he said, "I'm going to check in with a few people I know, and see what I can find out about that bridge."

"Will you keep me in the loop?"

"Absolutely, I will."

We turned into the quarry and Björn pulled over to the right. He got out of the car and began examining the different piles of rock and gravel, all of which I was sure he recognized, and likely knew exactly where they were sourced. I walked towards Ruby Sube.

I was startled when the door of the trailer opened and a beefy middle-aged man stood there scratching his chest and looking us over. His stained heavy metal T-shirt didn't quite cover the full terrain of his belly. He had on jeans and Kodiak boots, wore a red bandana on his head, and was sporting a healthy five o'clock shadow.

"Good morning," I called out to him. "I'm just here to take that Subaru wagon out of your way."

"Good thing too. I was gonna get her towed today," he said. "Sometimes people think this is a junkyard and that, eh. I gotta keep this lot clear for pickups."

"My friend didn't mean to leave it here for so long," I said. "He's not well. Did you happen to meet him when he parked in here?"

"I'm only here in the mornings and that eh."

"Where do you park?"

He used his thumb to point behind the trailer. "Harley."

"Right," I said. I wanted Sophie to be with us so I could hear her say, "Central casting."

Björn was walking towards us. "Björn Sorensen," he said to the man.

"Donny," the fellow said, looking down from the doorway. He hadn't moved.

"So, you manage the quarry?" Björn asked him.

"Helpin' out. It's construction season. Everybody needs gravel an' that eh."

"My friend and I just took a drive down to the end of the road," Björn said. "There's a brand new bridge that's been built down there."

Donny grunted. "They finally got that finished, did they?"

"It appears to be complete. In fact, there was a tanker truck crossing that bridge and coming back this way. Did you see it?"

"Nope."

"I wonder what a large tank like that would be carrying?" Björn ventured.

"Wouldn't know. Don't have any call to go down that way."

"Really?" I said. "But what about all those tanker trucks that wait right here in this quarry for their turn to cross the bridge? Haven't you ever asked those cowboys what they're up to?"

"I have no idea what you're talkin' about, miss. And anyways, I'm only here in the mornings an' that eh."

"Well, their ruts and tire tracks are all over the ground here," I said, looking around.

"So? This is a quarry. All kinds of trucks come in here to get slate and heavy rock. They turn around in here, they have trailers an' that eh—there's always tracks here. I never seen no tankers."

"No problem. We were just curious," Björn said, calming the waters.

"Let's hope this car starts," I said, moving towards Ruby Sube.

Donny belched, disappeared back into the trailer, and shut the door.

I got into the Subaru and turned the ignition. She started right up. Old reliable, I thought, relieved to be getting her out of there. I backed up slowly and turned so I could approach the quarry exit. Björn pulled further in, and I drove up alongside him for a quick word. Facing in opposite directions, we each rolled down our windows.

"Nova Scotia telephone," I joked.

Björn was serious. "So, what do you think, Roz?"

"What do I think? Either nobody knows and nobody cares, or everybody knows and they're all in on it. But one thing's clear, Björn. Nobody's talking."

Chapter 15

I was anxious walking into the Kentville hospital. What if McBride had taken a turn for the worse? But as soon as I rounded the corner into intensive care and saw Sophie's face, I breathed a sigh of relief.

"He's okay?" I asked

"He's still sleeping, but re-hydrating well. All systems go."

"I tell you, Sophie, he's resilient as hell. What do you want to do?"

"I'll just hang out, Roz. I'm fine."

"Okay, I'd better go and find out how Molly's doing at the vet's."

"Our two invalids."

"Living parallel lives."

"Then what, Roz?"

"Well, finding McBride was at the top of the list. Finding out what he knows is next. I'll call you later, and we'll take it from there."

When I got to Wolfville, I lucked into a parking space across from the vet's and went in. The young assistant who'd been there when I'd brought Molly in smiled. "She's doing better!" she said.

"Good news all round," I said.

"I'll get the vet." After a few minutes, he appeared in the doorway.

"Would you like to come back and see her?" he asked.

I nodded and followed him. Molly was lying down. He opened the large cage.

"Molly," I said softly. She lifted her head a little and her tail flapped weakly against the cage floor. I reached in. She licked my hand.

"What do you think?" I asked him. "Should I take her with me now, or leave her another day?" I was trying not to worry about cost. McBride would want what was best for her.

"Just resting like this and not being moved will mean she can continue to heal undisturbed, and we can keep observing her. I think another day would be wise. She's calm and needs sleep. And then, after she's out, she'll need a lot of care."

"Do you think she'll recover fully—that she'll be okay?"

"It will take time, but she'll be as good as new. She's a lucky girl," he said, looking at Molly.

Sophie was right, I thought, recalling her certainty that Molly would be fine.

"It could have been much worse if you hadn't gotten her here as soon as you did," the vet continued. "That wound was deep and badly infected."

Fear and anger welled up in me. I stayed a few more minutes with her, and then decided that I would take his advice and leave her there.

When I stepped outside, I spotted a bench further down the road, set in under two sheltering trees. I went and sat there a moment to take stock.

Danger at every turn, I thought, mulling over the tumultuous events of the last few days. Molly and McBride had each had amazing luck. Aurelia apparently had not, and as for Jacob, I worried that if things were to go awry with those thugs, he would not be spared.

My stomach churned. I leaned back against one of the trees and surveyed the town. To my right and a street over, I could see the peaks and domes of some of the campus buildings. I had a sudden impulse to visit the university library. The single entry in Aurelia's notebook had mentioned going to the library on the same day she planned to move up to her rented cabin on the Bay of Fundy. Since I now believed Aurelia and the girl in the tree were one and the same, I needed to find out what she'd been working on. It might shed some light on how she'd met her bizarre demise.

∽

I was amazed to find the library open. I introduced myself to Frida, the woman at the desk, and showed her my Public Prosecution Service ID. I asked her if they'd had a recent borrower or researcher by the name of Aurelia Strange.

"Oh yes—that young journalist!" she said immediately.

"That's right. I'm trying to track her down and I wondered if you have a local address for her, or if she left any kind of forwarding information."

"She was often here around the end of term. We were very busy at the time, so I didn't get to talk to her much. She used to sit at that table by the window over there, poring over things, making notes. But I haven't seen her for quite a while now. She's not in trouble is she?"

"No, but I do need to connect with her. Were there specific books or DVDs that she borrowed?"

"She wasn't one for taking books out. She was always working on material here, and that information wouldn't show up on her card."

"So she had a card?"

"Oh yes, she was registered…." Frida was looking at her screen. "Oh, I'm wrong—she did take out one book back in early May."

"What was it?"

"Naomi Klein's new book, *This Changes Everything*—just recently published. In fact she was its first borrower! She hasn't returned it yet and it's overdue. Oh and I see there's a change of address noted here. She moved from Kingsport to Old Mill Road."

"Old Mill Road." That morning Jacob had mentioned to Björn that he lived on Old Mill Road—according to him, a mere stone's throw from Caroline Beach and the cave that would now be forever burned into my brain.

Frida was writing down the address for me.

"And I've given you an email address we have as well. She didn't give us a phone number. I believe she's American."

"That's right," I said. "From Maine. So, apart from the Klein book, there's no actual record of what she was researching here?"

"No, I remember her diving into a lot of newspaper items and statistics and looking over maps, but I don't know what it was all about. Now, my colleague Genevieve might know— she helped her quite a bit. But she's away on vacation. Won't be back until next week. Why don't you come back then?"

"Thank you, Frida," I said. "I just might do that."

For some reason I felt less anxious. I had discovered once again that librarians tend to be the most helpful people in the world. I left the library and stood under the canopy of hardwoods on the campus grounds, looking at the address Frida had given me: 121B Old Mill Road.

I should go to Kingsport, feed the cat, switch cars, and then go over the mountain to this address, I thought. But first— should I visit the RCMP detachment and update Corporal Monaghan? So much had transpired since the previous evening when Constable Cudmore had found McBride's car. I was debating this when my phone chirped. It was Sophie.

"How's it going? How's McBride?"

"He's sleeping, but Roz—there are two men here to see him."

"Two men?"

"One of them looks like the guy who came out of the grocery store last night with Jacob."

"Sophie, it's them! Don't let them near him."

"The nurse won't allow visitors. Doris—she's pretty stern. She and I have bonded, so she's letting me sit with McBride. But they're out there, Roz. Waiting."

We rang off, and I stared up at the trees. I had no reason to assume their intentions were anything but lethal. I needed an ally—and someone with clout. On an impulse, I dialled the Halifax Police.

"Roz! It's been a while—how's the new job?" It was Detective Donald Arbuckle. McBride and I had worked closely with him on a previous case.

"I'm enjoying it, Donald, but for the present I'm on vacation in the Valley."

"Nice!"

"Yeah, only it's turning out not to be a vacation. Something's afoot and it's not good. I need your advice. Have you got a minute?"

"I'm all ears. Shoot."

I proceeded to give him a condensed version of the situation, starting with the day I saw the girl in the tree. "So now, there's McBride, lucky to be alive and hopefully recovering in the Kentville hospital, but Sophie's just called me with alarming news: the two heavies who accosted me that first morning are now lurking around the hospital trying to get at McBride. My guess is he saw something that day when he went back up the mountain. They failed to muzzle him once, and if they can get to him now before he talks, nobody will be any the wiser. I believe he's in serious danger."

"The Mounties should put a constable in the room."

"That's exactly what I would ask for, but according to Corporal Monaghan, so-called 'higher-ups' in the force are working with these same men. It's murky, but the cops seem to somehow be part of it."

"That's disturbing."

"No kidding."

"Okay, Roz—first things first. We've got a connection with a security firm in the Valley. I'll assign someone to his room today."

"That's a great relief! Drop me a text when the security person's in place. What's the company called?"

"It's called—hang on—Gateway Security."

"Thank you, Donald."

"I'm going to do a little digging around. We'll stay in touch."

I called Sophie. She answered softly. "Hi, Roz. McBride's still sleeping. I'm just stepping out into the hall."

"Are they still there?"

"I saw one of them nosing around the snack machine a few minutes ago. They've parked themselves in a lounge down by the elevators—I won't leave his side. I'm on guard basically."

I told her about my arrangement with Arbuckle. "I think he'll have someone from Gateway there soon, Sophie, so hang in. I need to take a little trip over the mountain, but I'll be at the hospital as soon as I can."

Chapter 16

I DECIDED NOT TO TAKE the time to go to Kingsport and within half an hour I was up over North Mountain and driving along Old Mill Road, which overlooked the Bay of Fundy. I parked across from 121B, the "little cabin on the Fundy side" that Aurelia had been so thrilled to find.

It sat close to the road and well apart from the main building, which was a modest '40s farmhouse with a screened-in porch. The cabin had a silent, deserted feel, but I rapped on the door anyway. Then—old habits—I tried to open it, but it was locked. Next to the door was a multi-paned window, with the blinds down.

I crossed the yard and went along the stone walk that led up to the farmhouse, climbed the front steps, and pushed open the screen door. Inside the verandah was a rickety card table with three rusty metal chairs, and an old wicker couch. The large main door to the house was locked. I rang the bell.

As I stood waiting, a young girl came bouncing up the porch steps and through the screen door. She jumped when she saw me. She was maybe twelve or thirteen.

"Hi," I said. "Sorry to startle you. I'm Roz."

She took a beat to get her breath. "Whatever. My mom's out."

There was no mistaking those startling blue eyes. Just like her brother's. Aurelia had been renting the cabin from Jacob's family.

"What are you staring at?"

"I'm actually looking for my friend Aurelia, the person who lives in your cabin."

"She left."

"She's moved?"

"She's away. Had to go somewhere."

"Oh really—when? I have something of hers."

"I dunno. A few days back." She shifted her weight.

"Do you know when your mom will be home?"

"After eight. She works at the hospital."

"In Kentville?"

"Duh." Gotta love the attitude, I thought.

"I guess it's the only hospital around here eh? What does your mom do there?"

"Cafeteria."

"What about you—aren't you supposed to be in school?"

"It's one of those 'teacher symposium days'." She made the air quotes gesture.

"Oh, right. What about Jacob? Is he around?"

"How do you know my brother?"

"From the arts centre. He told me where your house was. What's your name?"

"Katie."

"So Katie, would you mind letting me into Aurelia's place? I just want to sit for a minute and write her a note."

"I guess."

"I won't be long."

"I gotta find the key."

"Okay great, I'll meet you over by the cabin." I took out a notebook and pen from my shoulder bag so I wouldn't forget to actually write the note. My props, I thought. But my real intention was to get a look at the place. If Aurelia's things were still in the cabin, there might be some clues as to what she'd been working on.

Katie came loping across the grass. "Found it." She handed me a key on a bright orange lobster claw ring.

"Hall's Harbour?" I said, eyeing the key ring.

"Hey—how'd you guess?"

"I'll just be a minute," I said, smiling. She trotted away. So far, so good.

I entered the cabin and let the door click shut behind me. I locked it. With the blind drawn, the space was gloomy. I turned on the lamp that was sitting on the table, and set my notebook and pen there.

I got to work. It was a tidy one-room cabin. There was a single bed, made up, nothing under the mattress, and nothing underneath on the floor. There was an easy chair, a small chrome kitchen table with two matching chairs, and a door which led to a tiny bathroom. Some cosmetics and sundries were in the medicine cabinet, including a tube of lipstick, which I tucked into my pocket to compare to the other I had found. Next to the bed was a small closet with a cloth curtain hanging in front of it. I pushed it aside. There were clothes on the hangers, some boots and shoes on the floor. An empty suitcase was upended against the left-hand wall, and a knapsack was hanging from a hook on the right. I lifted the knapsack and it had enough weight to make me curious. I took it off the hook and poked through it. Inside was the Naomi Klein book from the university library—but more importantly, a laptop in its zippered case.

My heart was beating like a rabbit's. I hastily grabbed the computer and its adapter and slipped them into my shoulder bag. I took the Klein book as well and then placed the knapsack back on the hook. My entire search had only taken a couple of minutes.

I sat down and scribbled a note to Aurelia, telling her she had left her journal behind and how to reach me. I tore it out of my book and secured the corner of the note under the lamp.

I let myself out of the cabin and crossed to my car, making a show of putting my notebook and pen back in my shoulder bag as I walked, and casually dropping the bag onto the passenger seat. When I turned back toward the yard, I saw Katie sitting on the front steps. I walked up the path to give her back the key. "Thanks, Katie. What a sweet place. No wonder she likes it so much. I left the note on the table for her."

"Oh—there's my brother!" she said. I turned, and Jacob was pulling into the yard in his silver Honda. He climbed out and stood looking over the car door at me.

"You didn't have to track me down, you know. I told your friend Björn I had to go to work at the centre."

"Björn gave me the message, Jacob. I had no idea this was your place. Of course when I clapped eyes on your sister here, I knew where I was—you and she are the spit of one another. No, I'm actually looking for your tenant, Aurelia. I got her address from the library. Before she moved out here, she was renting the cottage I'm staying in. She forgot something there, so I'm trying to get it back to her. Katie mentioned she's away."

"Whatever it is, you can give it to me—I'll keep it for her."

"No, it's okay, I already wrote a note for her, left my info. Where did she go—back to Maine? That's where she's from, right?"

Jacob closed his car door. "We don't give out information about our tenants," he said curtly.

"Then again, maybe she's still around here investigating something. She's an award-winning journalist, right?"

"It's really not any of your business where she went."

"You seem edgy, Jacob. Is something wrong?"

"You've been in my face about stuff for days...I'm getting sick of it."

"You mean those three times I asked you if you'd seen McBride, or if you could tell me where to find a vet, or when I asked what you were doing coming out of that cave on the beach...or now, trying to find out where Aurelia went? Me getting out of your face isn't going to change anything. In fact, under the circumstances, I might be the best friend you've got right now."

"What's going on? What are you guys even talking about?" Katie asked, upset by the tension between us.

"Nothing! Go inside, Katie!" Jacob said.

"I don't have to—"

"JUST DO IT!"

Katie slammed the screen door and disappeared into the house.

"Look, Jacob, you're just lucky McBride's alive. I told you this morning I have to speak to the police about what we found in that cave. So just come clean about whatever you know—I'll vouch for you. I work in the legal system. It's better to have me on your side. Don't push me away."

"You don't get it," he said walking towards me. "Remember you said soon it would be too late? Well, the truth is, it's already too late."

"I'm listening."

"I can't. I can't talk to you. You have to leave."

"Okay—but this isn't going away. When you decide you're ready to talk, I'm there for you. So think about it. Here's my card." I held it out.

"Just go."

"It's your call." I set my card on the steps and walked past him, down the stone path to the road. I got into Ruby Sube. When I looked back at the house, he was gone.

My phone bleeped.

"Hi, Sophie."

"The Gateway security guy is here, Roz. I got him to show me his ID."

"Good…so how's McBride?"

"He stirs every now and again but he's not really coherent. They've got a sedative in him. Sleeping's probably best. Now that Clint—that's his name, Clint!—has arrived, I'll go get a bite in the cafeteria."

"Okay. If all's well on your end I'm going to run over to Kingsport. The poor cat's probably dismantled the fridge by now."

"Take your time, Roz. I'm fine."

"I'll see you soon—and Sophie…just don't say anything to anybody about anything, okay?"

"I'm like the grave."

I put the car in gear and headed back towards the Valley. I glanced at my shoulder bag lying on the passenger seat. I reached in and put my hand on the computer just to assure myself it was really there.

"I promise you, Aurelia Strange," I said aloud, "I'm not giving up. I'm going to find out what happened to you."

Chapter 17

WHEN I ARRIVED IN KINGSPORT, there was an RCMP cruiser in my driveway, parked behind Old Solid. I pulled off onto the grass and parked McBride's car in front of the roadside door. With my visitor in mind, I decided to leave my bag containing Aurelia's computer in the car. I locked it and walked around the cottage to the cliff-side.

"What's up, Corporal Monaghan?"

She turned from where she'd been knocking on the porch door. "Oh, Roz, there you are! I've got an update for you. We get dailies from Emergency Health Service, and two paramedics picked up your friend McBride on Caroline Beach this morning and took him to the hospital. I thought you should know."

"I've been talking to his wife. She's at the hospital. But thanks. Have you been able to find out what happened to him?" I said, hoping to suss out how much she knew.

"He's in no shape for visitors, so we haven't been able to ask him any questions."

"So you went to the hospital?"

"No. I called earlier. Have you been there?" she asked.

"Briefly. Long enough to be assured that he's stabilizing. It was a close call." She nodded. "Tell me, Corporal, have you got any new information about the girl?"

"Classified," she said. "You know that."

"I think you owe me one," I said. "I was right about McBride being in danger when I came to see you in Wolfville, and now we have the proof. I'm asking about the girl because I believe what happened to her and what happened to McBride are connected."

"The person who called the ambulance this morning was Professor Björn Sorensen. Do you know him?"

"Yes. Have you spoken with him?"

"Not yet," she said.

"Corporal Monaghan, it's time for you and me to hunker down and exchange information. We almost had a death on our hands this morning, so why don't you stop protecting whoever's being protected, and let me know what that 'classified' information is? We each know things the other doesn't. I'm not giving up and going away, so why don't we work together?"

"Look, Roz, I'm low on the totem pole. I don't even know what the classified information is. 'Classified' is not a joke. Orders come down from the top. I don't get to ask questions. I obey orders. That's how it works."

"Obedience is all well and good, but in this case, it amounts to aiding and abetting."

"You know that accusation is completely out of line."

"Is it? Did you know those two 'overzealous' goons that you're protecting are hanging around the hospital trying to get at McBride?"

She blanched a little. "How do you know that?"

"Because McBride's wife had to prevent them from getting into his room. So what about offering a little protection for McBride, for God's sake? At least tell me who those guys are working for!"

"I don't have that information."

"Come on! I'm not buying that!"

"They're American. That's all I can tell you."

"Just like the flag that was wound around that poor girl. It wasn't hard to figure out they were American. Tell me something I don't know."

She looked at her watch. "I have to leave—I have an appointment in Wolfville."

"With Björn Sorensen?" I asked as she walked back toward the cruiser.

"That's right. His class is over at five."

Fuming, I watched her disappear up the road. I needed to know what she was holding back. Björn had been anxious for me to talk to the police, so I knew when Corporal Monaghan interviewed him he would be forthright with her. Within the hour she would have all the details of what had gone down this morning on Caroline Beach. His information would include me being there as well as Jacob's presence when we discovered McBride in the cave.

Fortunately Björn knew nothing about Aurelia or that I had found her lipstick markings on the cave wall. If Corporal Monaghan was determined not to share what she knew, all my information about the girl would stay with me.

I went back to McBride's car to grab my bag, unlocked the cottage door, and went inside. The cat was right there. She actually looked thrilled to see me.

"Oh my gosh, you poor abandoned thing, you must be starving," I said. "Coming right up—breakfast, lunch, and dinner!"

I put the bowl on the floor. She was purring so intensely she could hardly chew. But she managed to gobble it all down in less than a minute.

"Okay," I said to her. "I'm going to do something radical. I'm going to let you go out." She looked at me. "It's guilt," I said. I opened the porch door and she stood quietly beside me for a moment, looking around. "Go ahead," I said. She bounded off the stoop. "Don't climb the tree!" I shouted, and closed the door.

Filled with anticipation, I took Aurelia's laptop out, sat at the big porch table, and opened it. The computer's battery had run down, so I plugged in the adapter. After a moment, the screen lit up.

Her desktop was orderly, but crowded. There was a large section of "Bee Files," no doubt her research for the award-winning article on "the lowly honeybee." There was another group of files on "Environment, Climate, and Disasters," all of which I wanted to read.

The file that caught my eye was called "Background—Fundy." I was about to open it when my phone bleeped. It was Jacob.

"Okay," he said.

"Okay, what?" I asked.

"I'm sorry about earlier. I thought about what you said, and you're right. I need to talk. Can we?"

"Oh, Jacob—I'm relieved to hear it. Do you want to come to my cottage at Kingsport? That's where I am now."

"I can be there within the half-hour." I gave him the address. We rang off and I called Sophie. She answered immediately.

"Is everything still okay?" I asked her.

"Just got back from the caf. The nurses are changing shift. Our friend Clint from Gateway is still here, so hopefully those creeps will eventually leave. I haven't laid eyes on them since I got back up here, but you can bet they're lurking. Oh, and McBride—guess what he's doing? Still sleeping! When are you coming, Roz?"

"There's been a little development—a breakthrough, actually. Jacob's decided he wants to talk to me, and I'm anxious to find out what he knows, and just how much trouble he may be in. He's coming to Kingsport. I might be a couple of hours."

"No worries. I'm right where I want to be—and I've got a good book."

I went back to Aurelia's laptop and sent the "Background—Fundy" file to myself. I was just starting to peruse other titles on her desktop when I heard a car pulling into the driveway. That was fast, I thought. Way too fast.

I unplugged Aurelia's computer and ran it up the ladder to the loft. I slid it under the double mattress. Then I looked out the loft window.

"I'm an idiot!" I said aloud.

It was Jacob all right, but he was in the Range Rover with the two suits, who had apparently given up on the hospital. Jacob's phone call to me was a trap and I'd fallen right into it.

Chapter 18

I watched the three of them start to head along the side of the cottage towards the porch door. I practically threw myself down the ladder, and just had time to grab my phone from the porch table before they were alongside the big windows. There was no chance to rescue my bag from the armchair. I darted into the kitchen and crossed to the roadside door. Same ploy as before, except this time I had neither McBride nor car keys.

I opened the door a crack. All clear. I could hear them banging on the porch door, and as it squeaked open, I slipped out the back, shut the door softly, and jumped off the stoop straight into the bushes. I slid under the wooden fence at the property line and dashed into the thick stand of trees clustered on the point—the very same trees where the murder of crows had been screeching their heads off the day this all began. There were bay laurel shrubs densely growing among the trees, providing me with decent camouflage; I crouched down in their midst to catch my breath and try to figure out my next move.

At that very moment, I heard another vehicle come up the road and stop. I recognized the peculiar engine putter of the old Mazda truck that McBride had 'borrowed' from the farmer.

A minute later there was a loud rapping coming from the ocean side of the cottage, the squeak of the porch door opening, and the farmer's voice as he called out, "Roz!"

I crawled back through the shrubbery until I was near the property fence again. From my vantage, I could see his Mazda parked across the road in the turnaround by the field. Keeping to the fence, I inched towards the seaside corner of the house, staying low and maneuvering until I could see the porch stoop through the weigela shrub. The farmer, Jeffrey, was still outside, standing there holding the porch door open. His golden lab, George, was at his side. He called out again.

"Hello?… Oh! Who are you?… I'm looking for Roz…. She's not? Well, I'm sorry fellahs—you can't be here if she's not in. You can leave a number and she can call you when she gets back…. Oh yes I do have a right! I own this place. So off the property now!" As his voice became louder and more authoritative, George joined in, barking loudly.

To my amazement, the men came out through the porch door with Jacob between them. They passed the farmer, and he watched them as they went along the front of the cottage and turned towards the road. At the corner of the house Jacob turned back and tried to say something but was yanked away by the other two. Then I heard the SUV start up and drive away.

I quickly scrambled under the fence and got to my feet.

"Thank you!" I called out, giving Jeffrey a start as he was about to round the corner of the house to make his way back to the Mazda.

He stopped and looked over at me. "What was going on there?" he asked. "Your friend McBride told me about these two unpleasant characters showing up the other day in a big black Range Rover, so when I saw that thing drive past my road a few minutes ago I decided to check it out, and sure enough this is where they landed. Now, I'm not sure what they're after, but I don't want any trouble here."

"Believe me, neither do I. They're serious bullies is what they are. They said they were here on 'official business' the other day, but they refused to explain themselves or show me any ID. They got pretty rough with me the last time, so when I saw they'd come back I hid over there in that stand of trees. Thank goodness you decided to check it out. You seemed to handle them just fine."

"I think it was George here that scared them off." George was now lying on his back with his legs in the air hoping for a belly scratch. "He's enough to make you shake in your boots, don't you think?"

"Yup, that's a terrifying sight," I said.

He cracked a big smile. "He's adopted, you know. Listen, if they come back, just call my cell—it's always on. George and I will take care of them. Come on, George!"

I thanked him again and went inside.

Despite the farmer's heroic declaration, I didn't feel safe as I looked around. Things had been overturned, drawers were open, and plates were pulled out of cupboards. The books from the shelf in the living room were lying topsy-turvy on the floor. I dreaded climbing up to the loft. I went up a few steps until I could just see over the plank floor into the space. Pillows were thrown aside and the mattress was flipped over.

Of course! Jacob must have discovered I'd taken the computer from the cabin. I'd been a fool, first to fall for his ploy about wanting to talk, and secondly, to think they were here to hurt me. So what did I do? I left the place wide open for them to search undeterred. No wonder they'd complied so readily when Jeffrey ordered them to leave. They had what they came for.

Aurelia's computer was gone and all I had was the one file I had managed to send myself. My bag had been dumped out into the armchair, but nothing seemed to be missing. The Klein book was lying open on the floor. I picked it up and turned it over. It had fallen open on pages 346 and 347 in the midst of a chapter on hydraulic fracking. Aurelia had folded down the corner of the page and in pencil she had underlined a sentence that began, "In 2012, the industry created 280 billion gallons of wastewater...." I closed the book and set it on the porch table. I decided to leave the mess for later. I got into Old Solid and headed for the hospital.

Just as I was about to take the Canard Road shortcut to Kentville, I spotted Björn's Volvo coming towards me on the highway from Wolfville. I pulled onto the shoulder and beeped as he passed me. He did the same on his side and I got out and ran across the busy road. He rolled down his window.

"More Nova Scotia telephones?" he said with a wry grin.

"One adventure after another, Björn. Did Corporal Monaghan catch up with you?" I asked.

"I just came from a short meeting with her."

"And?"

"She was surprised to learn that you and Jacob were on the beach this morning when we found McBride."

"I expect she was," I said. "She knew about McBride's situation because of the EHS ambulance call. The report would likely only include the caller and the patient, and possibly Sophie."

"So, you didn't fill her in?"

"I'll do that when she fills me in. She has information that I want. I was hoping we'd each come forward with everything we know, but so far she's not willing to do that."

"Well, Roz, I told her the truth as best I could."

"Of course, Björn. You did the right thing. And I'm sure she'll be back to see me very soon."

"It's been a long day. I'm heading home. How's the invalid?"

"That's where I'm going now. Sophie says he's sleeping a lot. He's a lucky guy, thanks to you."

"Don't hesitate to stay in touch. Try and get some rest."

Half an hour later I was in the elevator going up to McBride's floor. Sophie had her favourite wool shawl wrapped around her and was curled up in the armchair beside McBride's bed, sound asleep. Clint from Gateway was seated outside the room on a bench. I asked him if there had been any untoward activity.

"They approached earlier this afternoon, but they didn't get past me. Now it's all quiet. I believe they've left the building."

I nodded. "I saw them in Kingsport about an hour ago, " I said.

"Then the question is when will they be back. I've got a replacement coming in for the night. Will you need us tomorrow?"

"I'll see if I can find out what the prognosis is."

"Unless I hear otherwise, I'll be here."

I made my way down to the cafeteria, but it had just closed and the staff was cleaning up. "Not even a crust of bread?" I said plaintively.

One of the women shook her head. "All done for the day."

"Story of my life," I said.

Then from behind one of the stainless steel counters I heard another voice.

"There's a little soup here, dear. Beef with barley. If you don't mind it in a Styrofoam container."

"I'll take it gladly," I said, walking towards her. She was looking down, a kerchief around her hair, spooning out the soup, but as she looked up I saw the telltale sapphire eyes. "Are you Jacob and Katie's mother?" I asked, as she handed me the soup and a white plastic spoon.

"That's right, dear. I'm Darlene. Now how do you know my kids?"

"I met Jacob at the arts centre. And I saw Katie today out at your place—she told me you work here. I'd stopped by to leave a note for your tenant. I have something I want to return to her."

"If she doesn't come back soon, I'm going to have to turf her things. She only paid me to the end of last week. Where is she—do you know?"

"I wish I did."

"Well, truth be told, I'm glad she's not there."

"What do you mean?" I asked.

She leaned towards me over the counter. "Between you and me, dear, Jacob was getting in too deep. And she's a lot older than he is. You know what I mean. Nothing but trouble, for the pittance I charge for the place."

"He had a crush on her?"

"Oh my heavens, I'll say. Up late with her every night in that cabin. And then when her car gave up, he started driving her everywhere—I mean you can't really live up there without a car. And then he took it down to his mechanic buddy on Parker Road. Jacob will probably end up paying her bill because that car is fixed and just sitting in our garage now, and we don't know if we'll ever see her again. I tell you—do anything for her."

"So I wonder where she went," I said.

"I didn't see her leave. Jacob said he drove her into Kentville to get the airport shuttle—that she had to go somewhere for a few days. But then the heartbreak—oh yes! Crying in his bedroom, can you believe it? I don't know. Maybe she went to see her real boyfriend—or her husband, who knows? Or maybe she just told him she wasn't interested. But oh my gosh, the tears!"

"When did she go, exactly?"

"A few days back, it was. Less than a week. What's your name, dear?"

"Roz," I said. "I'm staying in Kingsport. I've got a friend in the hospital here."

She nodded. "Well, I gotta get all this stuff put away. I've got a ride coming."

"Thank you for the soup, Darlene. I was starving."

"Better you eat it than us throw it out." She disappeared through the swinging doors into the back area.

I was gobsmacked! So Jacob had been in love with Aurelia? A few days back would be around the time I'd seen the girl in the tree out in the basin. But when was she in the cave writing her name on the rock wall? Did he really drive her into Kentville to get the shuttle? And did she run into trouble after that?

I finished the soup and got back into the elevator. I nodded at Clint and tiptoed into the room.

Chapter 19

I was surprised to hear McBride's voice. "Hello, stranger."

"You're awake!"

"Which is more than we can say for this one here," he said, looking over at Sophie, who was still curled up in the chair, dead to the world.

"She had a busy night," I said. "As did we all. How are you? I thought you were a goner, McBride."

"You're not the only one…and Roz, I lost Molly."

"No, no. I got her! She's at the vet. She's recovering. Didn't Sophie tell you that?"

"Maybe she did…it's all a blur. I knew you both found me…I remember that. But I don't recall anything about the dog. That's good news."

"Sophie and I think you and Molly are living parallel lives as invalids. Anyway, I'll be picking her up from the vet tomorrow, and hopefully we'll get you out of here too, right?"

He had drifted back to sleep. I decided to head back to the cottage. I leaned over, and put my hand on Sophie's shoulder.

"Hey…" I said softly. "Soph?"

She opened her eyes and pushed herself into a sitting position. "Everything okay?"

"Yeah. I just thought you might like to get a decent rest— come back to the cottage. McBride's fine. He was just awake and alert for a few minutes."

"Oh no! I missed it," she said.

"I think he's on the mend. There'll be an overnight guard in place, so we don't need to worry. Anyway, you can take Ruby in the morning and be back here bright and early," I said.

"Okay—you're right." She stood and gathered her things. "It feels weird leaving, though." She put her hand on McBride's shoulder, and then leaned over and gave him a little kiss on the forehead. "Good night," she said.

I walked out into the hall. "Okay, we're getting ready to go," I said to Clint. "What time are you expecting your replacement?"

"Soon. I'll fill him in."

The sun was setting, creating a soft orange glow all through the halls. I walked along the corridor to the nursing station, and asked the nurse if McBride might be released the next day.

"The doctor wanted to wait on the decision. There'll be test results to consider as well," he said.

"Right, so what's the best time for me to see the doctor?"

"She'll be around most of the morning. It's Dr. Beattie."

"Here's my number if you need to reach me."

I walked back down the hall and met Sophie at the elevator.

"Let's find a restaurant," she said. "I'm starving. You never eat, Roz."

"How about the Port Pub?" I said. "Best pulled pork. Twenty minutes away."

"Done!"

"I can catch you up on the latest."

"Never dull."

"It'll be good to relax a little. It's been pretty intense."

The elevator doors opened. "Oh, thank God!" I said.

"What?" Sophie asked.

"I just had a mini-nightmare that the doors would open and those two thugs would be standing there gaping at us. I had a very unpleasant visit from them this afternoon."

"Really, Roz? There's just no getting rid of them."

"They're like shit on a shingle, Sophie."

"That's exactly what McBride would say! Like shit on a shingle." It was good to see her laugh.

She was still giggling as we stepped out through the front door of the hospital—just in time to see Jacob's mother, Darlene, climbing into the SUV.

"That's Jacob driving, isn't it?" Sophie said.

"So Jacob was her ride—but, Sophie—does this mean…"

"That the other two just got dropped off ? Your nightmare vision of them on the elevator! Maybe they were on their way up as we were coming down."

We whisked back through the doors. "I didn't really want that pulled pork dinner," Sophie said as we raced towards the elevators.

When we reached McBride's room, Clint was in conversation with his Gateway replacement, Andy. The floor was calm.

"We're not sure they're here," I told them. "It's possible that Jacob drove them somewhere else, and then used their vehicle to come and get his mom. Let me know immediately if either of them appears," I added, confirming that Andy had my contact information in his phone.

"I'll do a quick scout around before I leave—see if they're lying low in any of the usual waiting areas," Clint said.

"Dinner, take two?" I said to Sophie.

"I'm staying," she said, with that stubborn tone I knew so well.

"Up to you, Soph. I guess I'll be dining alone."

"I can't leave, Roz. Will you be okay?"

"Of course, you know me—tough as nails. Don't worry. Besides, I've got the cat. See you tomorrow."

✑

I picked up a small pizza in New Minas, and made my solitary journey back to the cottage. It was dark but there was a full gold-tinted moon just rising over the Minas Basin, its reflection reaching across the calm surface towards me. The cat, still outdoors, was sitting on the back stoop when I arrived, and the crickets were in full voice.

"Well, Smarty Pants, at least I won't have to organize a late-night search party for you," I said. "Bet you're hungry. Want some pizza?"

It was a relief to be in for the night, though the June bugs slamming themselves against the porch windows kept my adrenalin flowing. After we ate, I tidied up the chaos from the afternoon invasion and sat down on the couch with my phone, anxious to finally peruse the folder I had downloaded from Aurelia's computer.

My phone bleeped and I jumped. It was Mark from the Beckett troupe.

"Hey, how are you?" I said, surprised and delighted to hear from him.

"No—how are you?"

"What do you mean?"

"There was a little local news item about McBride being rescued from a cave on the Bay of Fundy, and taken to hospital. I had to call."

"Yikes, the media? That's all we need. I'm okay, Mark. It was nerve-wracking, but luckily we found him in time and he's recovering, so all is well. Sophie's camped out at the hospital. Listen, I've been meaning to get in touch with you guys. I think we should go ahead with our workshop idea for next week."

"Are you sure, Roz? Because we'd really like to do it."

"I'm sure. This is official!" I said, committing to the plan. I could feel the all too familiar pull between my two separate lives. "I've actually put a deposit down on one of the performance studios from Wednesday through Friday of next week. So you and the others could maybe drive up on Tuesday evening. That would give us three solid days to work."

"This is great news, Roz! We'll get everything rolling then."

"Maybe bring some mock-up props—always useful."

"Good idea. I'll go through the scripts and gather some stuff."

"Excellent! See you in a few days…and listen, Mark, thanks for checking in. I really appreciate it."

"We love you, Roz. We're not doing this project without you."

We rang off. I felt my spirits lift. "Really, life is short, Pussycat, and it's nice to have something to look forward to." She purred in agreement, and promptly fell asleep beside me.

"Must be all that outdoor exercise," I said.

I was just back to my phone files when I was startled by a sharp rap on the porch door. Looking through from the living room, I could see Corporal Monaghan standing on the stoop. "Not yet, Aurelia," I said softly as I set the phone down on the coffee table.

"You're working late," I said, opening the door.

"Some days are like that."

"Come on in, Corporal. What's on your mind?"

"You knew I was meeting up with Björn Sorensen this afternoon."

I nodded, and gestured towards the chairs around the porch table.

"Well, he told me all about the early morning rescue of Mr. McBride. And I understand you were there as well. You hadn't mentioned that when I saw you earlier, so I'd like to get your side of the story."

"Where should I start?" I said, taking the seat across from her.

"Just tell me what happened in your own words." She opened her notebook.

"Okay. Björn picked Sophie and me up here at 5 A.M. and he drove us out to the Fundy shore near Caroline Beach. You probably know the road is tricky to find. It's barely a road— more like a track—and that you pretty much have to go when the tide's out if you want time to see anything on the beach. That's why we went so early."

"Go on."

"Björn knows the caves in that area from a project he did with some students a few years back. So he led us along the shore until we came to the *Caroline* shipwreck monument and in the centre of the cove we could see a narrow crevice in the rock—like a fissure. Anyway, when we got up to the opening, someone was backing out through it—it was Jacob. I'd met him a couple of times up at the Jasper Creek Arts Centre." I hesitated, unsure about how many details to give her about Jacob.

"Then what happened?"

"McBride was in there all right. Jacob said he'd brought him some water. Björn called an ambulance and then went back up to the road to wait for it, and Jacob went with him."

"And what did you do?"

"I went into the cave to see how McBride was doing and sat with Sophie. She said that he'd come round for a moment when they took the restraints off his feet and hands. We waited for the ambulance."

"Okay. That all lines up. Except that Björn Sorensen told me the kid tried to run away when he saw you, and you ran after him, tackled him, and had an argument with him"

"Look, Corporal, the previous day, when I found Molly injured on the beach, I stopped in at the arts centre to ask him if he'd seen McBride. He claimed to know nothing. So when I saw him coming out of the cave and he bolted away like a startled deer, I was furious that he hadn't told me sooner where McBride was. I mean, for all I knew at that moment, it might be too late. So, yeah! I chased him down."

"What did he say?"

"He said he hadn't any idea that McBride was there until that morning, that he'd gone out early to check the caves along the shore. I asked him why he ran away from me. He didn't have an answer for that. But I do."

"What do you mean?"

"Okay, Riley—can I call you Riley?"

"Sure."

"When Jacob's not working part-time at the arts centre, he's working for those two so-called investigators that accosted me the day you and I saw the girl in the tree through your binoculars—the two 'Americans' that are somehow connected with the 'higher-ups' in your organization. He's chauffeuring, doing errands, and who knows what else! He's on the payroll! He might even be with them right now, because the three of them paid a little visit here this afternoon just after you left, and they tossed the place.

"And as I mentioned earlier, McBride must have stumbled on something incriminating the afternoon he went back up the mountain and disappeared, because those two have been skulking around the hospital waiting for a chance to get at him. The sorry state we found him in on the beach would indicate they don't mess around. They wanted to shut him up for good—and still do!

"Anyway, that's why Jacob ran from me, Riley. Because he's in too deep. I don't believe for a second he just happened to look in the cave. He knew McBride was in there. So that's what I know. And now I think I deserve to be told what you know. If it wasn't for Sophie and me and Björn, you'd have a corpse on our hands instead of a man recovering in the hospital."

"Let's back up a bit here. So you're saying they arrived here this afternoon and started ransacking this place right in front of you?"

"Not in front of me. I made a run for it when I saw who had pulled into my driveway. I'd already had a close call with those two, and I wasn't looking forward to another one. I hid in the trees the next lot over. Then the farmer who rents out this place showed up and told them to leave."

"Jeffrey did?"

"Yeah. And his dog, George."

"George, the golden lab who gets loose and likes to run down the middle of the highway?"

"So you've met George?"

"Well, it's a small place. I've had to arrest George a couple of times. He's kind of a traffic hazard and, well—" Riley started to chuckle—"a bit of a...well, a pedophile."

"What do you mean a pedophile?" I asked.

"Oh, you know. Little kids. George gets sort of obsessed when he sees one and likes to push them down in the garden or the field or on the beach. I mean he doesn't hurt them. He just sees a little kid and he can't help himself—next thing you know, over they go."

"Oh dear."

"Yup."

"I hear he's adopted," I said.

"Yup. The Mennonites across the road from Jeffrey's moved away and kind of forgot to take him along. Understandably." It felt good to share a laugh with her, even if it was at the expense of poor George.

"But seriously, Roz, I mean, what were those three looking for this afternoon?"

"I…assumed it was my phone, which is what they were looking for the first time, because it has the pictures of the girl and the helicopter recovery, which they saw me taking. The pictures haven't surfaced anywhere and I guess they haven't given up on getting them from me—to make sure they never do surface."

"But they didn't find your phone."

"No, luckily I'd managed to grab it just before I hightailed it outside."

"Can I see the pictures—I mean right now? I promise I won't forward them or anything. I just want to see them."

"Okay, why not?" I went into the living room and got the phone. I scrolled back to the beginning. The first picture was of the girl placed on her right side on the sandbar and facing out across the basin. I could see that despite Riley's stalwart demeanor, she was affected by the image. The sequence took us through the securing of the body, the lift up into the helicopter, and finally the departure of the helicopter to the north.

I was surprised to feel relief as I showed the images to Riley. Could I trust her enough to tell her about Aurelia Strange, that I was 100 percent certain I knew the identity of the girl? I could hear McBride in my head saying, "Keep your cards close, Roz. Don't play them unless you're sure it's the right move."

"So the chopper flew over North Mountain," Riley said.

"That's right, and that's the direction it had come from as well. And I have a theory about where it was heading."

"Which is…?"

"I told you about the bridge that McBride was standing in front of when we lost contact." I stood, and walked over to the window. "There's something up there, Riley, across that bridge and on the top of the bluff right on the coast. Something they don't want anyone to see. A place that's visited regularly by tanker trucks—maybe some kind of factory or something." I turned and looked at her. "I think that's where the helicopter went. Sophie and I were intent on hiking up through the woods this morning to try and suss it out, but we ended up tracking down McBride on Caroline Beach instead."

"Let's you and I go."

"What?"

"Tomorrow morning. Let's go find out what's beyond that bridge. This has been going on long enough. I'll pick you up at seven."

Riley's invitation was completely unexpected—and presented me with a tempting and much safer option for finding my way to the top of that bluff.

"What about the 'higher-ups'?" I asked.

"What about them? I don't have any instructions to curtail my movements."

"Okay Riley, you're on! See you at 7 A.M."

I stepped outdoors to watch Riley's cruiser disappear into the darkness. I'd been awake forever and felt desperate for a few hours of sleep, but just for a moment, I settled on the stoop and breathed in the balmy night air. The moon had turned to bright silver and was hanging like a charm in the night sky. "Bring us luck," I whispered.

Chapter 20

THE CAT WAS STANDING ON my pillow putting her paw on my face. I started awake. "For heaven's sake!" I said to her. Instant loud purring. Now that she'd had a taste of the great outdoors she wasn't about to waste time doing something boring, like sleeping. I looked at the clock. "Oh no." I leapt out of bed. It was 6:40. "Yikes—Riley will be here any minute! Okay, let's go." There was no shared moment of deliberation this time. She was off the stoop in a flash. "You're welcome!" I shouted.

I hastily dressed and washed my face. The images of the helicopter recovery were fresh in my mind from showing them to Riley a few short hours before. When I looked in the mirror to brush my hair I could see Aurelia Strange staring back at me, just as she had when I'd taken that first image of her on the sandbar. "I know," I said aloud, staring back at her. "I'm working on it—I've got Riley onside now."

I jumped as my phone bleeped. Donald Arbuckle. "Hi, Roz. Hope I'm not disturbing your sleep."

"The cat got to me first, Donald. Anyway, I'm almost out the door. Heading over North Mountain this morning. I'm determined to see what's on the other side of that bridge."

"Well, after McBride's close call, I'm sure I don't need to remind you to be extremely careful."

"Actually, I'll be with Corporal Monaghan, so I'm expecting to get somewhere."

"I'm calling to make sure that security service is working out for you."

"So far they're excellent! And thank you—because we did need assistance yesterday and Clint is smart and pleasant. He managed to keep the invaders out of McBride's room without trouble, and last evening as I was about to leave, I met Andy—his night replacement. I haven't heard from Sophie, so I'm assuming all is well. I'll let you know if McBride's able to leave today."

"Good. I put in a call to an old acquaintance of mine from out that way who's a regional superintendant with the RCMP. I'm going to see what he's got to say about all this 'classified' business and who those thugs actually are."

"So your RCMP acquaintance would be one of the 'higher-ups' then?"

"Well, possibly. His name is Dudgeon."

"As in High Dudgeon?" I said, laughing.

"Exactly."

A horn sounded in my driveway.

"Oh—there's my ride, Donald. Gotta go. Talk soon."

I fastened my seat belt, Riley handed me a takeaway from Tim's, and we headed off down Longspell Road. A few minutes earlier when I'd let the cat out, the bright sun had been climbing over the basin, but now a bank of dark clouds obscured the sky.

"Looks like rain," I said.

"It's overdue. Anyway, the farmers need it to get that hay growing. It's almost time for the first cut of the season."

"So what's the plan?" I said.

"Yesterday's EHS rescue puts McBride's case smack into my purview and since, as you reported, that bridge was his last known contact position, it's a legitimate place to start. Once we're there I intend for us to cross the bridge, and check out what's beyond it. After that, I'll go over to the hospital and see if McBride's alert enough for an interview."

I nodded and took a sip of coffee. I would have approached things the other way around—interviewing McBride first to find out what he'd uncovered rather than going in blind. Violent encounters had landed McBride in that cave at Caroline Beach and Molly at the vet's, not to mention the tragic demise of the girl in the tree. Whatever these guys were up to, it was no joke.

On the other hand, I was itching to get a close look at exactly what was going on up there on the bluff. I was grateful to have Riley with me, finally willing to take this on.

"Still blue sky over North Mountain," I said as we turned at the juncture and headed up the hill. Within minutes we had jogged over to Jasper Creek Road and were on our way down to the Bay of Fundy.

"That quarry's just ahead, where Constable Cudmore found McBride's car."

"Right," Riley answered.

"Slow down a little. I want to see if that guy's there."

"What guy?"

"Björn and I met him yesterday when he drove me down to pick up McBride's car. Donny, his name is. Says he works at the quarry in the mornings. We asked him about the bridge, but he claimed to know nothing about it."

"They're all the same, those guys."

"Are they?"

"Oh yeah—you can't pry a thing out of them, especially if you're a 'come-from-away,' which you are, being from the city. And don't forget, you're also a 'girl'."

"You wouldn't want to share any information with a 'girl'."

"Nope."

We were chuckling about this as she began to slow down. I couldn't see Donny anywhere, but it was hard to miss the tanker truck looming in the quarry entrance.

"Yikes," I said. "Just keep going, Riley. We can't risk the driver getting nervous about cops." I could feel her bristle at my giving the orders, but she kept the car moving. "Let's pull off somewhere along here. I know, take the cabin road that goes off to the left near the shore. I have stuff to tell you," I said.

We took the left and stopped just out of view of Jasper Creek Road. "Shoot," she said.

"Okay!" I looked at her and tried quickly to bring her up to speed. "I told you last night that there were tankers up on that bluff," I said. She nodded. "When Constable Cudmore called me about locating McBride's car, Sophie and I drove out to the quarry. While we were there, three different tankers used the quarry. We figured out that they were waiting their turn to cross the bridge. So that truck we just passed is either in a queue or maybe the bridge is just opening up for the day, but in any case he's waiting for a call."

"You've actually seen these trucks cross the bridge?" Riley asked.

"Yes. We followed one and watched him cross it and drive up onto the bluff, and yesterday, at mid-morning, Björn and I saw one come down from there and leave. In fact, he almost ran Björn over!"

"What do you mean?"

I told her about Björn's failed attempt to flag him down and find out what he was up to. "Honestly, we're lucky Björn's not in the hospital with McBride." I said.

"Maybe you and I will get the answer for Björn. What do you think? Should we wait until that tanker we just saw at the quarry crosses the bridge—or should we cross now?"

"Well, timing is everything...." I didn't have to decide because just then we heard the lumbering sound of the tanker approaching.

"That must be him," I said. "Let's leave the car here and go out to the road on foot. We can watch him from up here. That way he won't get spooked by the cruiser and once he's gone across, we can get the car and follow."

She tucked the cruiser off to the side of the narrow lane, and we walked through the trees to the road. A clap of thunder made me jump. We stayed on the shoulder. From there we could look down and see that the truck had stopped at the bridge. As we watched, the cable released and the tanker rolled across. Riley's attention was glued to the truck as it began to climb the steep slope to the bluff above.

I looked back to where the old fella normally sat. "Riley, look! That's Jacob down there manning the cable. See—he's working for them!" I looked down at the parking area and sure enough, there was his silver Honda.

Another huge crack of thunder was followed immediately by lightning and a torrent of rain. It was coming down hard. The two of us raced back to the car.

"Oh God," I said, slamming the door. "I'm soaked through."

"Me too. But it won't last."

"You don't think?"

"No—you can see it moving. Look at those clouds whipping out over the bay."

"Why don't we go see McBride now, and then come back after he's given us the lowdown? By then, this rain will have moved on. 'Forewarned is forearmed,' right?"

"That's a good old adage, Roz, but mine is 'Strike while the iron is hot.' I want to see what that tanker's doing up there on that bluff right now. I mean, we're here, let's do it. How long do you think we have? How long does it take to empty a tanker of that size?"

"From my research—depending on the quality of the pump—it's about 350 gallons per minute, so if it's 10,000 gallons it would take about half an hour to pump it out, and from what Sophie and I have been able to observe, the tankers aren't up there for long before they're signalling to the next one."

"Let's get going!" Riley said. She began to back around in the pelting rain. We pulled out onto the main road. The wipers were going a mile a minute and I could barely see, but Riley had no problem negotiating the pitched slope. She turned right and drove the twenty yards to the start of the bridge. The cable was secured, but Jacob wasn't there.

We sat there in the pouring rain. Riley beeped her horn. I looked down into the little parking lot and could see Jacob through the rain-streaked windshield sitting in his car. "He's not moving, Riley. Just sitting there."

Riley, impatient, backed the cruiser up until it joined with the road that ran down into the parking area. We drove down and pulled in beside him.

"This kid is not going to stop me from getting across. He'll do what I tell him!" she said.

Now I could see that Jacob was on the phone. "Who's he talking to?" I said.

He signalled to indicate she should wait a minute and continued talking. After what seemed like forever, he put the phone away, put the hood of his slicker up, got out, came over and stood by Riley's door.

She lowered the window and the rain blew straight in at us. "Corporal Riley Monaghan, Jacob. I need to cross that bridge."

He bent down to see who was riding with her and our eyes met.

"Please go on over there now and release the cable for us," she continued, hollaring over the din.

"Everything's closed," he hollered back. "The storm! It's too dangerous to climb the hill in this rain. You'll have to arrange to come back another time."

"I'll be fine on the hill. Now release the cable, Jacob."

"It's a safety issue!" he yelled.

"I take full responsibility. Let's go, or I'll have to charge you with obstructing an officer."

"Go back and wait by the bridge. I have to clear it first."

Riley reversed and turned around to go back to the bridge. Jacob was on his phone again. Perhaps sending a warning that the RCMP was on the way up.

"Obviously in a lot deeper than running a few errands for those guys," I muttered, more to myself than to Riley.

"We'll deal with Jacob, Roz, but one step at a time. I hope we're not too late to see what's going on up there. It's already been at least twenty minutes since the truck went in." We stopped in front of the cable once again. "That's got to be a tough climb for those heavy trucks. I wonder what they're carrying—or maybe they're loading something into the trucks up there...no, that doesn't make sense, does it. What the hell is that kid doing?" She leaned on her horn.

The rain was letting up. Riley opened her door a little. I followed suit. The lightning flashed over Cape Split as the storm moved out to sea. We both pushed our doors wide open, got out of the car, and stood waiting on either side.

There was a screeching engine sound from behind us. It was the Honda.

Jacob pulled up along the driver's side of the cruiser. He got out.

"What's going on, Jacob?" Riley called over to him. "The rain's letting up. Let's go!"

He walked around the front of his car, and came and stood next to Riley. I joined them. "Your visit wasn't pre-arranged," he said. "I've been instructed to make an appointment with Corporal Monaghan to visit another time, and to ask you both to leave immediately for your own safety." I could see he was trying to sound calm and managerial but he could barely catch his breath.

"We're here now and we'd like to get a look at the operation, and a proper understanding of what's going on up there," Riley said, pointing at the top of the bluff.

"Yes, and we'll arrange for you to do that at a better time. For now, let's clear the area."

"Nice try," I said.

"It's for your own protection," he countered.

"Protection from what?" I asked.

"It's an industrial site. It's not safe for members of the public to be up there."

"I'm not the public," Riley interjected. "And neither is Roz. She's a private investigator, and a partner to Mr. McBride, who as you know, Jacob, may have been assaulted while investigating this location."

"Exactly. We don't want to see any more injuries. So you need to leave now," Jacob said.

"Look," Riley said, "I'm going to try not to construe what you just said as a threat. But only if you give us the opportunity right now to see what that tanker is doing up there. And I want a sample of whatever he's carrying. Otherwise I'll be compelled to call on the Department of Environment, and you can tell your bosses it often takes them months to check things out. In the meantime, they might order a shutdown. So it's in everyone's best interest for you to help us out now. And then, presto! We'll be out of your hair."

"If you insist on seeing anything now, you need to have a warrant. Do you have a warrant?"

Riley stared back at him. I knew she hadn't had the time to get a warrant.

Suddenly there was the roar of an engine and the tanker emerged from the trees at the top of the bluff.

"Dammit! Now it's too late," Riley said, directing her annoyance at Jacob. The trucker slowly negotiated the incline and then drove onto the bridge and stopped in front of the cable. He gave a couple of beeps and put up his hands up in a gesture of exasperation at our cars blocking his way.

Jacob signalled for him to wait a minute.

The sky was a bit brighter, and I took out my phone.

"While I'm here, I just want to get a couple of shots," I said.

"Absolutely not allowed," Jacob said.

I quickly took a picture of the tanker waiting on the other side of the cable. Then I took one of Jacob. "Not bad," I said. "You look kind of grumpy though. Should I post it?"

"Stop this!" he said. "Why can't you be reasonable?"

"Reasonable, Jacob? Think about it! You called me yesterday and said you wanted to come and talk to me and tell me everything. I was so pleased and relieved. But it was a trick! You showed up with those two creeps and turned my house upside down and stole Aurelia's computer!"

"Back! I stole it back! You were the one playing games. Tricking my sister into letting you into Aurelia's cabin so you could 'leave a note for her'—so sweet and friendly! And then stealing her computer and who knows what else! I had every right to come and take it back from you."

"No. You needed it back because it's chock full of evidence about what's going on here. That's what Aurelia was research-ing. She had discovered exactly what this place was all about. That's why she came here in the first place and that's why she's dead, isn't it? She was killed for what she knew!"

The waiting trucker lost patience and started leaning on his horn.

"All right! That's enough," Riley yelled over the din. She looked at Jacob. "Tell your bosses I want an appointment for an official visit. And I expect it to be soon. So get that ar-ranged immediately. Otherwise, I will be back with a warrant. I also need you to come in for an interview, Jacob. You've got some explaining to do about your involvement on Caroline Beach, and your part in illegally entering and ransacking Roz's cottage yesterday. I'll be contacting you to set that up."

Jacob turned abruptly and got into his car.

We got into the cruiser and Riley put it in gear and backed away from the bridge. "And you, Roz! What was that big speech you gave me yesterday about how we should be shar-ing information? All this Aurelia stuff is news to me. I want to know exactly who she is and what you're talking about!"

Chapter 21

"You already know who Aurelia is," I countered, as we headed back along Jasper Creek Road. "You saw her through your binoculars, wrapped in the flag, tangled in the roots. Aurelia is the girl in the tree."

"No one knows who that girl is, Roz. She disappeared in a helicopter before she was identified."

"It's a long story, Riley, but I have evidence that the girl whose pictures I showed you last night is Aurelia Strange. She's—she was—an environmental journalist. She came up here from Portland, Maine, to pursue an investigation. I still don't know how she wound up dead, but after seeing the state McBride was in when we found him, it doesn't surprise me. In fact, I'd say you and I are lucky to be safely out of there as we speak."

"So what was all that about you stealing her computer?"

"Eventually she ended up staying at Jacob's mother's cabin—that's where I found her computer. I had it in my hands long enough to see she had files on her desktop labelled "Fundy." Then Jacob arrived with his two nasty pals and, like I said, I was out of there. I'd hidden it, but I should have kept it with me. I blew it. I was afraid they'd come to rough me up or something, but they'd come for the computer and, like a dope, I left the place wide open for them, and they found it."

"It's evidence. We can seize it."

"Maybe, but they've likely destroyed it."

"What else?"

"What do you mean?"

"What else about Aurelia?

"I can barely stand to think about her. She graduated from King's a few years back. Just this spring, she won an emerging journalist award in Maine. She believed the prize money was meant to bring her back to Nova Scotia. She was smart and talented and enthusiastic and she died for no reason other than her work to uncover some greedy scheme."

"You think they killed her?"

"Unfortunately, we don't have the luxury of an autopsy—they made sure of that. But…yes, that's what I think."

"So what goes on with those tankers? Do you know?" Riley asked.

"That's where McBride comes in. He may have found out, and paid the price."

We had begun driving down the highway into the valley. "We need to talk to him about all this. I'll head for the hospital," Riley said.

"Let me call Sophie first." I took out my phone.

"Hey, Soph! How's everything?"

"McBride's doing a lot better, Roz. Almost normal."

"He was never normal, Sophie. Listen, I'm with Corporal Monaghan and she needs to ask McBride some questions—should we come now?"

"He's scheduled for a couple of tests this morning, and then they'll decide whether to release him."

"Okay. Let's stay in touch then."

"Roz? Don't forget Molly."

"Right. I'll get her. Thanks." We rang off.

"So, no interview yet. McBride's having tests. Can you drop me back to Kingsport? I need to get his car, and then go pick up Molly in Wolfville."

We turned onto North Medford Road and drove towards the coast. The sky was clearing over the Minas Basin.

"I'll go back to headquarters to do some research on the Jasper Creek location—rattle some chains, see if there were any permits issued for whatever is going on up there. I mean, helicopters, tanker trucks, electronic cables—it's not exactly a Mickey Mouse operation. It must have been inspected."

"Björn was shocked when he saw that bridge. Neither he nor his colleagues knew anything about it."

"My guess is they'll never make that appointment for me to look the place over. I'm going to set to work on getting a warrant ASAP," Riley said.

We turned onto Longspell Road. Grace was set up across from the farm by the side of the road on a camping stool with her watercolours and her easel.

"Another world," I said.

"You got that right. It's like a dream out here."

Riley let me off at my cottage. The cat was on the stoop. "Time for lunch?" I asked. Her tail twitched and she leaped off the stoop and disappeared into the dense brush on the other side of the fence.

"Okay then," I hollered after her. "I'm going out to eat!"

I got into McBride's car. Why not get a bite in Wolfville? I barely had a crust of bread on hand, anyway. I drove back along the road and when I reached the farm, Grace sig-nalled for me to stop. I pulled over and crossed to where she was set up with her easel.

"How's everything, Rosalind? Björn told me about your friend who was rescued from Caroline Beach. Is he all right?"

"The two of you seem to specialize in beach rescues," I said. "McBride is recovering, thank goodness, and he may get out of the hospital today. His wife is with him—you met her the other day."

Grace nodded. "Oh yes, Sophie."

"That's right." I was circumspect, not knowing whether she was aware of Björn's long-ago romance with Sophie.

"Björn has some information for you," Grace said. "Something about the bridge. He had to go teach this morning, but he mentioned wanting to get in touch with you."

"I'm heading in now to pick up McBride's dog, so maybe I can track Björn down on campus."

"Here, I'll give you his numbers." She wrote them down on a scrap of watercolour paper and handed it to me. "There's his cell, and the second one is his office number."

"Perfect. Thanks Grace. I love your painting." She had perfectly captured the spirit of a litter of piglets frolicking in the farmyard with the sows in the background, lolling in the mud.

"I paint the pigs all summer. They sell like mad. Those sows just turn out one litter after another. Soon this bunch we're looking at will be teenagers and there'll be more little ones. That Boris is a busy boy."

"Boris the boar?"

"Well-named!" she said.

"And so handsome!"

I got back into Ruby Sube and continued on to Wolfville. The vet's office was just down the road from a new Italian café. I parked in the lot across the road. As I walked towards the café, the door opened and I recognized the woman who was leaving.

"Frida?" I said.

"Oh yes—Roz! Listen, my colleague Genevieve will be back next week and I know you were interested in talking to her about Aurelia's research."

"I'd love to meet with her. On Wednesday I start working on a Beckett project, so will she be back before then?"

"She'll be back Monday. What is the Beckett? Genevieve and I are both fans. Is there a performance?"

"Most likely we'll have a staged reading next Friday evening at the Jasper Creek Centre. I can let you know. It's short dramatic works."

"Here's my card. Oh, and I have Genevieve's here too with her email address. So let us know. Back to work!"

I went into the café and ordered a sandwich and a cappuccino and decided to sit on the patio in the sun. I got out the numbers Grace had given me.

"Professor Sorensen," Björn answered immediately.

"Hi, Björn. It's Roz. How are you?"

"Very good, and you?"

"I'm well, Björn. McBride might be released today, and I'm in town to pick up his dog. I saw Grace. She mentioned you might be looking for me."

"Yes. Yes indeed. I've been doing a little checking to find out who's behind that monster bridge and what its true purpose is."

"And?"

"Well, first of all, it was built for a completely different reason—oh, excuse me, Roz, there's a student here to see me. Office hours, you know. Anyway, I will talk to you soon. Maybe Grace and I will take a walk up the road and drop in later."

"Please do. I'm intrigued," I said.

My sandwich arrived and I was so thrilled just to look at it and to know that I could eat it. Lunch! A rare event. It was perfect. I ate every crumb, finished my cappuccino, and headed up the road to the vet's.

Molly gave a little woof when she saw me, and began batting her tail vigorously against the cage frame. She seemed much stronger.

"Now for the real pain," I said, getting out my credit card.

"I know. They should have Medicare for pets," the assistant said.

"We'd mortgage our houses for them, though, wouldn't we? I can't tell you how grateful I am to see her so alert."

"Once they start to mend it's kind of miraculous."

"Thank you, and please thank the doctor for me."

We left the vet's and stepped into the sun.

"Now go slow, Molly-girl," I said. "No dancing."

It felt good to have her with me. Molly had always been easy company. I opened the passenger door of Ruby Sube and she climbed up onto the seat as she'd been doing since she was a pup.

My phone bleeped.

"What's the latest, Sophie?"

"The patient is cleared for departure!"

"Really! Well! I was going to take Molly to the cottage, but I'll come straight to Kentville. What's happening with the Gateway Security guys?"

"Clint is here, bless him. He'll stay until McBride is safely on his way, and he said he would let Arbuckle know they're done here. So far today, there've been no sightings of Flopsy and Mopsy."

I laughed. "Finally, some names that really suit them."

"Courtesy of Scary Doris the night nurse."

"See you in twenty minutes."

"Don't bother to park, Roz. We'll be down by the door watching for you."

Chapter 22

As Sophie promised, she and McBride were ready and waiting outside the main doors of the hospital. McBride shed a few happy tears when I let Molly out of the car, and then we all climbed into Ruby Sube and made our way back to Kingsport.

McBride dozed off partway there. "Yup—he still sleeps a lot," Sophie said.

"You must be exhausted yourself," I said. "You didn't exactly have a proper bed."

"I don't know what I'm running on, but right now I feel great. Relieved, I guess."

"I'll get in some food later and we can have a real dinner tonight. They sell chickens and pork and greens at the farm. Maybe Björn and Grace would like to join us…or would that be too much?"

"No, it sounds good. I'll prepare it with you, Roz. I think McBride would appreciate being able to break bread with the man who helped to save his life. So, have there been any new developments?"

"Lots has happened, but the best news is that I think I finally have an ally in Corporal Monaghan."

"Good, because McBride and I talked about driving into Halifax early tomorrow. We need to go home."

"Did I hear my name?"

I looked in the rear-view mirror. I was shocked to see how drawn McBride's face was. "Good timing! We're here. I'll put the tea on."

Half an hour later we were all relaxing in the Adirondacks, taking in the mid-afternoon sun. Remarkably, even the cat and dog seemed content, as they stretched out together on the stoop.

"This is what a vacation's supposed to be like, isn't it?" I said, forcing myself to chill. I was chomping at the bit for details about what happened to McBride—but he deserved a moment of peace before digging it all up and reliving it—revolving it all, as Beckett would say.

Just then Grace and Björn appeared in the driveway with their two dogs.

"Join us!" I said. "Would you like some tea?" I stood quickly, preparing to take Molly indoors, away from whatever doggie fray might ensue—but miraculously all the animals stayed calm, as though an instinctive understanding had passed between them.

"No to the tea, thank you," Björn said. "We're just on our walk and we saw the cars. I was hoping you would be out of the hospital." He reached out to shake hands with McBride.

"I'm on the mend, and I understand that's largely thanks to you."

"Well, I helped Sophie and Roz find their way to Caroline Beach, and that terrible cave, but it was really Sophie who was leading the charge." He smiled across at her.

"Have you been able to recollect what happened to you, Mr. McBride?" Grace asked.

"I've often been in the wrong place at the wrong time, but this one takes the cake, and yes, as for what happened, the details are fuzzy, but it's starting to come back to me."

"Earlier today," Björn said, "I mentioned to Roz that I had acquired some information on that Jasper Creek site. Shall I fill you in?"

I looked at McBride. He nodded.

"Please," I said.

"Well, the industrial bridge and the gravel road that climbs up to the ridge were constructed almost two years ago by a communications company to prepare for the installation and maintenance of a new cellphone tower. However, that plan was scuttled—something to do with the signal not transmitting consistently. I'm not surprised, by the way— the magnetic properties of that ancient rock formation are unique and more powerful than we might think. Apparently the telecom people found a place further inland for the new tower.

"I would wager that by the time these tanker trucks start- ed taking advantage of the bridge and the road, no one was paying attention to that abandoned, isolated site anymore. I can find no official permits on record. The current activity, whatever it is, may be legal, but it's more likely happening 'under the radar,' as they say."

McBride nodded. "A covert venture that will last as long as they can get away with it."

"However," Grace added leaning in, "it's not unheard of for some nefarious bureaucrat to craft himself a little sweetheart deal should the opportunity present itself."

"Right," I said, looking at Grace in a new light. "McBride, I need to know what you saw, and what happened up there. Are you up for telling us about it?"

He stared a moment at the ground, as though attempting to unearth the memory. "I can try," he said, looking up at me.

"You called me from the bridge, to tell me about it, but we lost the connection…so then what did you do?"

"I remember looking up at that hill and thinking: why not? Just check it out…that's right…so I ducked under the cable, and Molly and I crossed the bridge for a quick hike to the top of that bluff. The sun hadn't set. I figured I had at least an hour of daylight.

"What about your car?" Sophie interjected. "What did you do with it?"

McBride shook his head. "I don't remember moving it. I must have left it parked just there…by the road that leads to the bridge."

"Constable Cudmore located it the next day in the quarry," Sophie added, "several kilometres from the bridge."

"It's lucky that fellow Donny didn't dismantle it and sell it for parts, eh Roz?" Björn said.

"I think we rescued it just in time, Björn," I said, and turned back to McBride.

"Our next lead was Molly's water dish," Sophie said. "Roz found that in the trees bordering the quarry."

McBride was silent, his brow furrowed. "Maybe when they stashed the car, they threw the dish there on purpose. So anyone searching for us might think that we had hiked into the bush and gotten lost."

"That makes total sense, McBride." I was growing impatient with everyone's interruptions. "Anyway—there you were, taking a quick hike to the top of the bluff with Molly…."

"That's right. I remember her sniffing around, happy for the run. Once at the top, I didn't see anybody up there, except for this one tanker truck driver—Eddie, I think…yeah, that's what his name was. I guess he assumed I belonged there. In any case, he welcomed the company."

"So what did you find out?" I said.

He closed his eyes. We all stayed silent, waiting. Then he looked at us. "Basically there's an opening in the ground up there—a hole. They've safeguarded that opening with a metal surface—a sort of large steel plate. There's a pipe fitting in the centre of the plate that the hose from the tanker truck connects to. Originally, it must have been dense spruce, but they've cut a circular road through the trees so the trucks can turn around, park, divest their load, and then drive straight out again.

We all looked at one another.

"Wow," I said.

McBride nodded. "It's a straightforward system…remarkably simple," he said.

"Yes!" Björn said, excited by the revelation. "These openings are what you'll find referred to on geological maps as 'vaults' and this big one you saw up there is known as the Jasper Creek Vault. There are others all along the coast—a natural phenomenon. The inside shape of the vault is a large underground cavern, which doesn't deteriorate because it formed within the basaltic lava when it erupted 200 million years ago, creating North Mountain. It's virtually indestructible. The Jasper Creek Vault extends down to below sea level and then runs horizontally deep underground and out into the Bay of Fundy."

"So, what exactly are these people up to, McBride?"

"Well, when I first got up there, Eddie was monitoring the pump on his truck which was sending gallons of stuff into the opening. I asked him whereabouts he lived, and he said he was from Ohio—made a couple of trips a week up here. I asked him who he worked for and he mumbled something about freelancing."

"But did you ask him what he was pumping?" I asked.

"I remember I asked him if the stuff could explode. He said he didn't think so, but that sometimes it smelled pretty strong…. He said all the drivers have a saying when people ask what they're carrying. Now wait—what was it? Oh yes, they say, "You wouldn't want to drink it."

We all looked at each other.

"So what exactly is it?" I said.

"That's what I said, Roz. I asked him, 'What exactly is it?' And he looked like he was about to tell me—but right then, that's when Molly was attacked from out of the blue by this vicious German shepherd and all hell broke loose. I ran over to rescue her, and the next thing I knew, a couple of big galoots were beating the crap out of me.

"When I came to on the floor of that cave, I was tied up—I could taste blood, I was bruised all over—could hear the tide but I couldn't see—I thought I was blind—was sure it was only a matter of time before I'd drown in there." He paused, struggling with the force of the memory.

Finally, he took a breath and looked at us. "You know the next part of the story better than I do, because by the time you found me I was down for the count. Anyway, Eddie from Ohio never had a chance to answer my question. I wonder what the heck happened to him."

Björn and Grace got to their feet, and she went over to the stoop to get their dogs. "We're very pleased you're on the mend. Between us all, we'll get to the bottom of this—and hopefully find a way to put a stop to this madness."

"Oh, before you go," I said, "Sophie and I were thinking we could make dinner for everyone. Would you like to join us tonight for a meal?"

"No, no, no—why don't you all come to us for dinner? Please! Let us have you as our guests," Grace said. "How about eight this evening? That will give everyone a chance to take a rest this afternoon."

I looked at Sophie. She nodded. "I'd love to join you for

dinner. Sounds great!" she said. "And a rest is exactly what I need."

McBride chimed in, "I'd like that very much."

"We're on then," I said. "Thank you, Grace!"

"We'll see you later." And with that they departed, dogs in tow.

Sophie got Molly and took her into the cottage to feed her, and said the two of them would take a nap.

"Feed the cat too, Soph!" I said.

McBride and I refilled our tea cups and moved our chairs across the grass to catch better sun.

"So you must have a theory, Roz." McBride looked at me.

"I think I have a good lead," I said. "I'm certain I know who the girl was." I gestured at the basin.

"The girl in the tree?" he said.

"Yes. Her name was Aurelia Strange. She was a young journalist. I've even found evidence of her being in the same cave where they dumped you." I got my phone and opened the photo I had taken of the lipstick letters marked on the cave wall. "I found the lipstick too. It was on the floor of the cave. I think they did the same thing to her as they did to you—only she ended up wrapped in a flag, tied into that tree, and floating into the Minas Basin."

"Crikey," he said. "Even with me at death's door in that cave, there you were sleuthing away!"

"That part about death's door is true—check out this picture I took of you in the cave."

For once he was speechless. "Anything else I should know?" he said, after a beat.

I told him about Jacob—his involvement with the thugs and us finding him just leaving the cave when we got there. "He said he'd been giving you water. Do you remember that?"

He shook his head. "No…I think I was pretty far gone by then."

"I'll say you were. So, back to Aurelia." I proceeded to fill McBride in on everything I had learned about her, and my recent foray into her cabin, where I'd found her computer and taken it. "Then Jacob called to say he was on his way over, that he'd decided to open up and tell me everything, which I'd been coaxing him to do. Within minutes he arrived, but it was a ruse—he'd brought the evil twins with him. So I quickly hid Aurelia's computer and hightailed it out of here for fear they'd rough me up again, but they turned the place upside down and found it."

"So you lost the chance to find out what she was researching."

"Exactly, and believe me, I was not happy that I'd fallen for Jacob's ploy. But as luck would have it, McBride, I did manage to get one file before they stole it back."

"Have you read it?"

"Nope, I haven't had a minute to myself—I guess I've been saving it for you!"

"Well, come on, Roz! What are we waiting for? Let's get at it."

Chapter 23

I WAS ABOUT TO OPEN the file when a call came in from Inspector Arbuckle.

"Donald!" I said. "I'm sitting here in the sun with McBride. He's on the mend! He's out of hospital, so that would complete the arrangement with Gateway. How's this working money-wise? Is it costing you or me or both of us our life savings?"

"All taken care of, Roz. As I told you we have a long-standing arrangement with Gateway and a budget to hire surveillance in special circumstances. And since I've begun to look into the situation myself, it's legit. I mentioned the last time we talked that I was waiting to hear from an RCMP regional superintendant from out that way."

"Right! High Dudgeon?"

Arbuckle laughed. "Well—it's Peter, actually. Anyway, it turned out he was coming into Halifax, so we met this morning."

"And—did you find anything out?"

"Well, you think you know people…. He was friendly enough at first, but not forthcoming, and then he got his dander up, told me I shouldn't be nosing around in a jurisdiction that I have no authority in, and I disagreed: I'm investigating on behalf of a Halifax citizen who suffered a very serious injury and ended up in the Kentville hospital. So we had a bit of a set-to. I was surprised at his reluctance to even discuss the situation with me. In fact, the attitude I encountered today which was supposed to drive me away has piqued my interest."

"'The lady doth protest too much, methinks.' Could he be covering something up?" I said.

"I guess that Shakespeare's good for something, eh?"

"Seems to have known a lot about how deception and corruption work."

"Anyway, I asked him why they weren't at least looking into it, and he told me he'd recently assigned Corporal Monaghan to the case."

"Corporal Monaghan said that the case is within her purview because of the Emergency Health Service rescue. She didn't mention being assigned it by a higher-up. But I think she's a good cop who wants to get to the bottom of this as much as I do."

"How did it go this morning at the bridge?"

"We got stonewalled—like you. Corporal Monaghan was told she would need an official invitation or a warrant—neither of which we had. On top of that, it was raining cats and dogs. Anyway, my bet is we'll soon be on our way back up there with a warrant."

"Keep me in the loop, Roz."

"I will. Also, McBride and I are about to look at something that may shed light on the whole operation. I'll get back to you if we have a breakthrough."

"Give him my best." We rang off.

"Donald didn't get anywhere with his old pal from out this way, who's one of the higher-ups," I told McBride.

"So what do you think?" he asked.

"I think everybody has their price—apparently even higher-ups."

"Or maybe especially higher-ups."

"Why doesn't anybody ever offer *us* a big bribe?" I said.

"Just lucky, I guess."

"Yeah. We just get beat up."

"And dumped in a cave."

"Yeah."

"Okay—let's get to work," said McBride.

I picked up my phone and opened the file. "Should I just read it out loud?" I said.

"Why not. I'll take notes."

"Do you need a pencil and paper?"

He tapped his temple. "Up here—notes up here."

"Speaking of notes, I haven't told you we found Aurelia's notebook right here in this cottage. Ellie spotted it in the loft the afternoon they were all here. In fact, you could say the cat found it. That notebook was my first clue that the girl in the tree and Aurelia were one and the same. Inside it was a clipping about her winning an award for environmental journalism, and her only entry was about preparing to move from here to a place on the Bay of Fundy. So you see, McBride, they're the same person!"

"Okay—so the notebook was your first indication. What else do you have?"

"The woman who sold her the book described her as having red hair. I know, lots of women have red hair, but that's not all. When Sophie and I studied the pictures I had taken of the girl, Sophie spotted a King's signet ring on her finger, which is exactly where Aurelia Strange studied journalism. And most importantly, I can feel it, McBride. I know it's her."

"If I didn't know you so well, Roz, I'd dismiss that."

"That's a roundabout way of admitting that I'm nearly always right."

"Are you going to read or what?"

"Here goes. You ready?"
I began to read.

Notes Re: Fundy Connection

Aurelia Strange

How 'Fate' brought me back to beautiful Nova Scotia:
I finally got to be in the same room with Naomi Klein. She
was in Boston on her book tour for *This Changes Everything*.
What an inspiration she is—brave and uncompromising. She
does tireless, exacting research and then writes and speaks
about her work in a way that fills me with urgency and purpose. I wish I could have a one-on-one meeting with her right
now to ask her advice. I've stumbled into an explosive story,
but people I know could lose their livelihood and worse. So,
as a professional journalist, how do you find the courage to
stick to your guns?

Background: Recent Investigation:
Celia was my family's housecleaner for years while I was growing up in Portland. She has a daughter, Lainie, who's about five
years younger than I am. People in Nova Scotia would refer
to Lainie as "a hard ticket" because she's been in and out of
jail a few times for minor infractions, but I always found her
more naïve than tough, and I like her very much, though she
drives me up the wall with her frequent bad decisions, and
her terrible taste in boyfriends. But recently, she hooked up
with a new man—Fuller—and her life seemed finally to take a
turn for the better. They're happy together and Fuller makes
a good living. "Even my mother likes him," she said to me.

"So what does he do?" I asked her. She beamed and told me
he's an international truck driver.

"That's impressive," I told her, "but he must be away a lot of the time."

She said they were mostly short hauls from the eastern US to Nova Scotia. "But he gets at least two trips a week and it's excellent pay—in cash! Even if it is kind of scary."

I told Lainie I couldn't see how going to Nova Scotia could be scary.

Her lengthy reply went something like this:

"Scary because, for one, he uses an unofficial border crossing into New Brunswick—it's someone's farm in Maine—and because, for two, after he crosses the border he's supposed to put a fake Nova Scotia plate on his truck, so he has to be super careful to make sure he won't get stopped. But really, it shouldn't be that scary since the place is like totally isolated, and most of the crossings happen in the middle of the night."

In a trice I went from being happy for Lainie, with her wonderful new guy who made a decent living, to being very, very worried that Fuller was deep into ongoing illegal activity.

"What kind of truck does he drive?" I asked, trying to stay calm.

"It's a big tanker. It takes special training for that kind of license, and Fuller is super qualified."

"But why cross illegally into Canada?" I asked her. "What's in the tanker—milk, gas, pesticides, chickens...?"

"No-no. Nothing like that. Chickens! You're funny. It's just water."

"Is there a water shortage in Nova Scotia?" I asked her.

"I don't think so," she answered, as though I was sadly lacking in intelligence.

"Okay—so what's it for?" I said.

"You got me," she said.

"Well, where does he take it in Nova Scotia?"

"Someplace up on Fundy where they built a thing for it."

"What kind of a thing?"

"All I know is he empties the tank, comes back across the border, and goes and fills up the tank again. Easy-peasy! Anyway, he's not the only one. There's a whole bunch of truckers doing it."

"But where do the trucks go to pick up this water?"

"Different places."

"You mean different states? Which ones?"

She shrugged.

"But they're close, right—didn't you say the eastern states?"

"I forget."

Lainie clammed up. Too many questions. And surely Fuller had warned her not to talk about his late-night border-crossing gigs, but these are the kind of slip-ups Lainie is prone to, especially if she's bragging about something or someone.

So I let her be, and promised myself that I would beg, borrow, or steal the money to get myself to Nova Scotia to do some serious digging into this tanker mystery. The gods were with me! That same week I won the Emerging Investigative Journalist' award for my article on the assault against the bees.

Fate was taking my hand and leading me back to my roots! That prize money was meant to pay for my new investigation at the Bay of Fundy.

I looked at McBride. "Risky business with the trucks. But what are they actually up to?"

"It correlates perfectly with that encounter I had with Eddie from Ohio. Roz, you need to find out exactly what they're doing up there, and then nail whoever's in charge of the whole thing."

I stood up and walked towards the edge of the bluff and looked across the basin. "And Aurelia, McBride. How did Aurelia end up out there?"

"You'll find out, Roz, like you always do. You'll figure it all out."

"Thanks a lot, McBride! This was supposed to be my vacation—and I've got the Beckett. I know you couldn't care less about my theatre stuff, but that's what I came out here for. And what do you do? You get yourself beat up and almost die on me…and now you and Sophie and Molly are just going to swan off to Halifax and leave me here with a murdered girl who won't get out of my head, while I try to tackle this major environmental crime that seems to be going on under everybody's noses!"

"Chill, Roz. You're not alone. You and Corporal Monaghan can get to the bottom of this thing. Or just walk away from it. Go ahead! That's what they're counting on—that no one will actually do the legwork and nail them."

"Goddammit!"

"Where are you going?"

"To make a cup of tea!"

"Make one for me too."

Chapter 24

McBRIDE AND SOPHIE LEFT FOR Halifax the next day, and I spent the weekend shifting gears and focusing on the upcoming Beckett workshop. Early Monday morning I was sitting in the porch reading Beckett's *Play*, trying to figure out what we could use in the workshop to substitute for the three urns that the characters are trapped in—stools? Large boxes?— when I heard the sound of a car in the driveway. Surely not the actors landing on me a day ahead of schedule…. But it was Corporal Monaghan who came around the corner and up the steps.

She opened the porch door and waved a paper at me. "I was the first one there this morning. The judge was barely awake."

"The warrant!"

"That's right—so are you coming with me?"

"No time to waste!" I said, grabbing my bag and jacket. And I meant it. A day from now I intended to be completely absorbed in the Beckett project.

"I know more about what's going on up there now," I said as we approached the turnoff to the mountain. "By the way, was this case assigned to you by the regional superintendent—Peter Dudgeon?"

"Hardly. That's not how it works, Roz. He's got bigger fish to fry. Why do you ask?"

"I have a cop friend in Halifax who was talking to your superior on Friday. Apparently he said he'd assigned it to you."

"I can't think of a single time he's actually assigned a case to me," Riley said. So McBride's gone? I wanted to interview him when he got out of the hospital. You were going to keep me posted."

"He needs recovery time, Riley—he and Sophie left Saturday morning. But he told me what happened to him up there."

I proceeded to catch her up on McBride's account of events.

"So McBride was assaulted immediately after he observed that tanker pumping something into a hole that leads to the Bay of Fundy?"

"That's right," I answered.

"Well, whatever they're up to today, it will be us that catches them in the act." She held the warrant up and gave it a shake.

∽

We were well along Jasper Creek Road. We passed the quarry. No tankers—at least not yet. We were soon approaching the end of the road.

We eased over the slope and turned right onto the gravel road that led to the bridge.

I leaned forward. "What the…Riley?"

"What?"

"Is it just me or…where's the cable? Has the electronic steel cable been removed?"

She stopped the car halfway to the bridge and we each got out and stared at it.

"You're right! It's not there, and look on top of the posts— the cameras are gone."

The crate the old codger used to sit on next to the cable post was not there either. The parking lot down by the fish shacks was empty. We looked at one another.

"This is totally weird," I said.

"Well, at least there's nothing stopping us from crossing the bridge. Let's go on up there and see what's what," she said, and started moving back to the car.

"Riley, wait! Either everyone and everything is gone or this is some kind of trap. Were they expecting you?"

"Not unless they were informed that I got the warrant, which is unlikely, and it was barely an hour ago."

"Should we get backup?"

"I think we should just drive up to the top of the bluff and take a look around."

I relented. "Okay—let's do it."

We got back in. She put the cruiser in gear and we headed across the bridge. The steep hill was tricky with deep ruts from all the tanker travel, but Riley maneuvered around them with skill.

"Not bad," I said.

"It's all those Valley back roads, Roz—lots of experience."

Finally at the top, we drove onto the flat of the bluff and paused. The gravel road continued ahead through the trees. The spruce stand was so dense it was like peering into a dark cave. Looking to our left, I could see the edge of the bluff and out over the bay. The narrow point of Cape Split was directly across the water.

"Let's get out and walk," I said, remembering McBride's detailed description. "I want to get a first-hand look at the target of all those tanker trucks."

Riley pulled over to the right side of the gravel road and tucked the cruiser in close to the trees.

"Gotta leave room for all the traffic," she said.

We got out and walked along the road for a bit. It suddenly widened into a large clearing and there was the defined circular track around the pumping area.

"So it looks like the tankers turn here, hook up and pump, and then they're facing in the right direction to go back," I said. "And it clearly is a set-up that works for only one truck at a time." We looked more closely at the steel plate with the connector in the centre that the drivers could attach their pump hoses to.

"So as Björn described it, this metal plate sits over a hole on the surface of the basalt rock. The hole opens into a large cavern, or "vault," which extends down below sea level and empties into the Bay of Fundy."

Riley took out her phone and photographed the steel plate and the connector.

I looked around. "According to McBride, right near here is where Molly was attacked by the German shepherd. McBride ran over to rescue her, and that's when he was grabbed and severely beaten."

"It's quiet enough up here now," Riley said, looking around.

"Eerily so," I said. "Feels like they're gone."

"Let's keep walking." On the far side of the circle, the road continued through the trees. Riley stopped in her tracks. "Now look at that!" I followed her gaze. She was looking at an open area near the edge of the bluff.

We walked towards it. "I know exactly what that is," I said.

We were looking at a 12-by-12-foot square aluminum platform about 5 feet high with cross-braced adjustable legs. Painted on the platform were three red arrow-like symbols that crossed in the middle.

"That is a temporary touchdown pad for a helicopter."

"Bingo. Your theory was correct, Roz. This is where the helicopter was heading," Riley said, taking a photo. "But if they're gone, why would they take away the cable infrastructure from the bridge, but not this?"

"A hasty departure? Or they're coming back for it," I said.

"Or maybe it belongs to a different company that will come and pick it up."

"Maybe. Let's keep going. See if they've got anything else up here."

We continued along through the spruce along the shadowy road; it had narrowed to a single track but was still wide enough for a car.

"I'd always imagined they had some kind of warehouse or headquarters up here, but there don't seem to be any structures," I said, peering around.

"Keeping it simple," Riley said, "in case of having to make a hasty exit. Look, Roz—see that enormous boulder up ahead? Look just beyond it. Is that a car parked on the other side of it?"

We hurried up hill towards the boulder. The car was tucked in—almost completely hidden. It wasn't a car I knew. We got up behind it and looked at the plate. *MAINE*, it read, and underneath in smaller letters, *Vacationland*.

"Holy crow," I said.

"What?"

I looked at Riley. "This must be Aurelia's car."

"Aurelia Strange?"

"That's right," I said.

"But what's her car—"

I interrupted her. "Can you hear that sound?"

"What sound? All I can hear are the waves hitting the shore."

"It's coming from the other way—not from the bay."

I stood still and listened. Riley did the same.

"It sounds like…."

"Digging?"

I squeezed between the side of the car and the boulder. Behind the boulder was a narrow path that travelled inland away from the main track. I began moving along it trying to get closer to the sound. Dense foliage and broken tree limbs were lying across the path, but the sound was getting clearer. There was a dip in the land and the path went steeply downward into a copse of hardwoods. I crouched to see better. Riley did the same.

We peered down through the leafy branches of the maple and ash trees and I could see the flash of a shovel glinting in the sunlight, and what appeared to be the shirtless back of a man, digging frantically.

I lay flat on my belly to get a better view through a gap in the trees. At that moment the man threw the shovel aside and began to claw at the dirt with his hands, pushing it out of the way until some muddied ragged fabric began to appear. It was unmistakable: the American flag.

I watched him reach into the earth and begin to lift the lifeless body of a girl.

"Oh God," I whispered. "Oh God, Riley!—It's Jacob, isn't it? She's there! Aurelia's buried there."

He gradually pulled her body free, lifting her out of her muddy grave.

Not even thinking, I was on my feet and running down through the trees towards him.

"Jacob!" I called. "Jacob, what are you doing?"

Startled, he looked up. He was sitting just to the side of the grave now, leaning against the gnarled trunk of an elm, his arms and upper body streaked with dirt. He held her, facing him, and pulled her body close against his chest. "Get away!" he called. "Leave us alone!" His voice was hoarse and he was out of breath.

"Jacob, it's okay. Talk to me—tell me what's going on."

"They can't just get rid of her like she never existed." His blue eyes darkened and he stared intently at me.

"No they can't, Jacob. That's very wrong." I crouched down a few feet from him. Riley kept her distance, up above us, and watched silently.

He had his right arm across her back, holding her against him, and he placed his left hand on her cheek. "She was so beautiful."

"She was," I said.

"And they killed her."

"Who did? Who killed her?"

"I warned her…she didn't know how dangerous it was…I tried to stop her from going, but she said it was too important."

"So you found her…?"

"I had her car—I'd gotten it fixed for her. I parked a ways up the road from the restaurant so I could see the door. I wanted to surprise her and drive her home after the dinner. But when they came out they had her between them."

"There were two of them?" I said.

"Steve—the CEO, and the other one, the older guy—the cop—I'd seen him at things over the years."

"So they had her between them," I said, "and then what? What happened next, Jacob?"

He grew silent, just looking at her.

I waited and took a deep breath. I could smell the pungent stench of death, mixed with freshly dug earth. "Tell me Jacob."

He looked into the distance. "They pushed her into the back of Steve's fancy rental, and drove off…."

He'd become still and much calmer. The harsh tones had gone from his voice, and he spoke with a distant, trance-like quality. He began to stroke her hair. "I followed them."

"They didn't see you?" I asked.

"They took her up the mountain. I thought they were taking her home."

"You mean, to her cabin?"

"But at the turnoff to Jasper Creek Road, the SUV was there...waiting for them. I parked in someone's driveway and watched. They pulled her out of the back of his car—she couldn't seem to walk at all—they were just kind of dragging her across the road. Like a rag doll—then they pushed her into the SUV."

"Then what?"

"Steve and the cop left—they headed back down towards the valley. The SUV drove past me and turned down the next road towards Fundy. It was getting dark. I stayed well back but I saw them turn off onto the narrow track to Caroline Beach. I parked her car in the trees by a deserted camper and ran the rest of the way down to the shore. I started to climb down onto the sand when I heard their voices in the distance—coming closer. I hid in the rocks."

"What did you hear?"

"One of them said, 'The tide will take her. She'll be gone in the morning.'"

"Was she in the cave?" I asked.

"The tide was running—they must have put her right into the water. It's taken me a long time to find her, but now I have, and I'm never letting her go." He wrapped his arms more tightly around her in a gruesome embrace.

Chapter 25

RILEY DID A MAGNIFICENT JOB of getting all of us off the bluff. She had an ambulance come to remove Aurelia's body, and arranged for her car to be taken to the police lab.

She led Jacob toward her cruiser. "You're coming with me to the detachment," she told him. "We've got some business to take care of." Riley was determined to get to the bottom of this case, and seemed willing to take on the higher-ups if necessary.

She had Constable Cudmore drive me back to Kingsport, and I called McBride when I got home and filled him in on the events of the morning.

"So they've skedaddled out of there, eh?" he said. "Maybe that visit you and the corporal paid them the other morning was too close for comfort."

"And maybe the fact that both Riley and Björn started checking to find out what permits they had was too much pressure. Anyway, they've cleared out…gone like the snow on the water," I said.

"Guilt can do that. Will you follow up with Arbuckle on what Jacob said about someone from the police being involved at the restaurant meeting?" McBride asked.

"Yup, I'm calling him next. Arbuckle can step in where Riley can't. She's willing to take them on but she's in an awkward position, obviously. Jacob's a mess, McBride. He's been sitting on all this. He'd clearly fallen hard for Aurelia. And he must have been afraid. He'd seen those thugs in action, although they now seem to have vanished with the rest of them."

"And good riddance to them! I still have scars."

"How are you doing?"

"Molly and I both slept in today."

"What's Sophie doing?" I asked.

"Right now—she's vacuuming."

"I see."

"Don't get on your high horse, Roz. I washed every dish in the house when we got here. The place is starting to look like home again. How are you?"

"I can't wait to escape from all this madness and dive into Beckett for three days with my company. Speaking of which, let me talk to Sophie for a minute."

Sophie came on the line. "Listen," I said, "I've been thinking about Beckett's *Eh Joe* piece that you wanted to work on. If we end up doing a little invited reading on Friday evening, would you come up and read the last section of it for us? I know the company would be thrilled to have you join us."

"In a heartbeat, Roz. I'll get started on it."

"Thank you. I'll let you know how our plans shape up."

Next I called Donald Arbuckle and told him what we'd learned from Jacob's revelations about Aurelia's death.

"And Jacob's certain that the man having dinner with Aurelia and the CEO was with the police?"

"Yes. Jacob said he was older, and that he'd seen him over the years at various events, but he didn't give me a name. Mind you, I didn't interrupt to ask—it was all just pouring out of him. I mean, there must be lots of photographs of the senior officers in this area that we can show him."

"Leave it with me, Roz. I'll be back to you soon."

❧

Riley arrived around four thirty, and she brought a pizza with her. "I know you have no food," she said.

"Björn and Grace sent me home with the leftovers after we had dinner there Friday night but I consumed every last bite over the weekend. So I'm starving now. You're an angel. Do you want some tea—or a hit of the Irish with your pizza?"

"Water's good."

"How are you, Riley? How did everything go this afternoon?"

"We got Aurelia's body to the medical examiner. On first look they've indicated she doesn't appear to have been beaten. From Jacob's account, they may have drugged her. We'll know in a couple of days. I took a statement from Jacob. Protocol is to keep him overnight in lock-up, but considering the shape he was in, I decided to take him home."

"I think that was best," I said.

"I dropped him off a couple of hours ago. It's his mother's day off, so she's there to give him a meal and sort him out. And I'm working on getting a search warrant for that cabin Aurelia was staying in."

"There's nothing in there," I said, "apart from a few clothes—unless Jacob put her computer back, in which case, it would be invaluable. Flopsy and Mopsy probably ate it. I hope Jacob's okay. Maybe I'll see him this week if he's working at the centre. You know I'm rehearsing up there right? You could come to the reading on Friday night if you like."

"See what you're up to. Make sure you're not breaking any laws."

"You never know. They're a rough crew."

"And they arrive tomorrow?"

"That's right, and then Wednesday through Friday we're at it. Take another piece." I pushed the pizza box towards her.

"No thanks. I should hit the road. I've got some paperwork to do at the detachment before I call it a day. I'm wiped. I was getting that warrant pretty early this morning. So can you forward those notes of Aurelia's that you said you have?"

"Let's do it right now," I said.

"Good idea. Get it over with."

I picked up my phone and Riley gave me her email address. I sent her the one file I had downloaded from Aurelia's computer.

"Got it!" Riley said, after a few seconds. She scrolled through her other messages. "Holy shit!"

"What?"

"Just a second, Roz, I have to call Constable Cudmore." She looked at me. "This can't be true."

He picked up and she spoke quickly. "Hi—tell me! Okay when? On what? ATV news—an actual clip? Okay, let me see if I can track it down. You're there now? I'll get back to you."

"What is it?" I said.

"On your phone, Roz—quick! Track down the 5 o'clock news—ATV."

"Okay…. Got it, I think….What are we looking for?"

"It's Jacob's place! Jesus Christ!"

"What?"

"I should've kept him in the lock-up!"

A banner scrolled across the screen: *Breaking News: Abduction from North Mountain.* Jacob's mother, Darlene, and his sister, Katie, were sitting on the wicker couch in their front porch being interviewed by a reporter from ATV.

"Two big men!" Darlene was barely holding it together as she spoke. "They roughed him up bad and pulled him right out the house and then they took off. We were some scared…. Katie, show them! She's got it on her phone."

The next thing on the screen was Katie's shaky video, taken through the porch window, of the helicopter in the front yard of the farmhouse. One of the thugs was pointing a gun towards the porch, and the other was shoving Jacob into the helicopter. Then they both climbed in and it lifted straight up and flew off to the south.

The reporter came back on saying, "Our team happened to be covering a funding announcement down the road at Baxter's Harbour. We were just on our way out when we saw the chopper taking off and we came over to investigate. The RCMP arrived a few minutes ago. There'll be more on this abduction. Tune in to the ATV late-night news at eleven." The item closed with a shot of an RCMP cruiser pulling into the yard, featuring Constable Cudmore at the wheel.

Riley was already back on her phone to Brad Cudmore. "Should I come up there?... Okay. It doesn't sound like there's anything more you can do. Did the perpetrators leave anything behind?... Well, check around. The mother and daughter don't need medical assistance or anything?... Find out if Jacob said anything to them about what was happening or if the abductors said anything—and take notes. And make sure you get a copy of the clip from the girl's phone. Did you hear me, Constable Cudmore?... Well, it helps if you say yes after I ask you to do something, then I know you've heard me. Okay, signing off. See you at the detachment."

She sighed. "He means well."

Riley left, and a horrible black cloud of guilt and utter helplessness swept over me. What fools we were not to see that coming. Now it seemed so obvious: the temporary touchdown pad for the helicopter still there, us assuming that everyone was gone including the two thugs. Of course Jacob was vulnerable. And his abduction this afternoon was a clear sign that he was in far too deep, that he knew who was involved and what they were up to. These guys hadn't disappeared—they were still cleaning up.

Chapter 26

MY PHONE BLEEPED. I STARED at it. *Harvie* flashed across the screen. "Really?" I said aloud.

Harvie Greenblatt had been working as a lawyer for the Public Prosecution Office in Halifax when I met him and had been instrumental in my getting a research job there. We had gotten close and were flirting with the idea of living together, but I was hesitant, ever leery of commitment. And then Harvie got offered the job in Montreal and we both took it as a sign that we should go our separate ways. But I had to admit, I missed him.

I picked up. "Harvie?"

"Roz—yeah hi. Hi! Roz, how are you?"

"Not great…I—"

"Not great? Oh no. I thought you were on vacation—isn't that what you said?"

"I am on vacation, and I'm doing the Beckett project, but I've gotten sidetracked into this terrible investigation. And earlier today I thought it was finally resolving but it's actually getting worse…. How are you, Harvie. Are you in Montreal?"

"No—well, that's the thing, Roz. I'm here. I'm at the Halifax airport. Just waiting on a car rental. I have a speaking engagement tomorrow night, a fundraiser thing for Dal Legal Aid organized by a longtime colleague of mine. Anyway, I thought maybe–"

"Yes!"

"What?"

"Yes! Come out and see me. Come right now. The Becketters don't get here until tomorrow evening, and a visit with you is exactly what the doctor ordered. I'll forward directions to your phone. It's about an hour and a half from the airport."

"Good, good. Wonderful! Okay. Is there a grocery store? I can cook something for us when I get there…Roz?"

"Sorry—I…."

"You're not crying?"

"With happiness, Harvie. Really, you're going to cook something?"

"Of course I am."

"Well, there's a big store just off the highway in Windsor and a well-stocked store in Canning that stays open until ten. But you'll have to get literally everything you need—I mean—I do have salt and pepper here. And oats. And I have some Irish whisky. But that's it. Oh and Harvie, could you pick up a couple of cans of cat food?"

"She's with you?"

"She's having a much better time than I am."

"Okay, Roz. Send me those directions. I'll be there before dark! Probably around eight. Take it easy."

"I will."

"Roz?"

"Yes?"

"It's nice to hear your voice."

We rang off. I forwarded him the directions and looked at the cat.

"Harvie's coming to visit us!" I said, feeling elated at the prospect. "And he's going to bring you some food. So do you want the last of those crunchies?"

I'd been holding them back so she'd have something for the

morning. She was all for having them now. She marched into the kitchen and stood by her dish.

"Okay, but go easy—don't forget to chew."

I paced around, full of anxiety about Jacob and impatient for Harvie's arrival. Today of all days I really needed a friend.

To calm my nerves, I stepped outside. I looked out across the Minas Basin, and was immediately overwhelmed with images of Aurelia on the sandbar, where all this had begun. I turned away from the view. The cat was at the porch door so I invited her to join me on the stoop. She came out and washed her face. The sun would be shining across the fields from the west for another three hours, so to shake off the dread, I decided to take a walk.

I went along the driveway to the road and turned right. I looked down and there was the cat beside me. "Want to come down to the end of the road and visit the cows?" I said.

Just where Longspell Road curved and headed north toward Ghoul's Hollow was the community's Little Free Library mounted on a post in the turnaround.

I unlatched the small door to see what treasures were in there. The book that caught my eye was called *Sea Sick* by Alanna Mitchell, and it was about acidification—the ocean in crisis. Sophie once told me that it had been developed into a powerful theatre presentation performed by the author. She had been deeply affected by it when she saw it in Toronto.

As I stood in the turnaround perusing the book cover, I recognized Björn's green Volvo coming up the road. The cat and I headed back towards the cottage and met up with him by my driveway.

"Björn! How are you?"

"Very well, thank you, Roz. I see you've chosen my book."

"Really—this was yours? I should have guessed."

"So how is our invalid doing?"

"He and Sophie left Saturday to go back to the city as planned. McBride told me today that he's been getting rest. I think he's out of the woods. Thanks again for that delicious dinner on Friday night."

"Roz, I came up here to tell you Grace saw a disturbing news segment on TV today, about young Jacob. Apparently he was abducted right out of his mother's house and removed in a helicopter. No one even knows where it was heading."

"I saw it too, Björn. Corporal Monaghan and I watched it. One of her constables went out there to Old Mill Road to investigate. Jacob knows too much and if they see him as a threat—well, just as they did to McBride, they'll do whatever it takes to shut him up."

I was unexpectedly in tears.

"Roz! Are you okay? You need a break from all this."

"I'm okay. Sorry. I'm just worried sick about him. I don't know what do about it…and that's always the worst."

"And weren't you planning to do a theatre project this week?"

"Yes, Björn, I still am. The actors are coming tomorrow. I better pull myself together!" I dabbed my eyes. "Don't worry, I'll be fine. I have an old friend coming up this evening for dinner."

"Please call on us if you need anything."

"Thank you for thinking of me, Björn."

He started his car and pulled around to head back. I watched him drive away.

"He has a kind soul," I said to the cat.

True to his word, Harvie appeared at 8 P.M. I helped him bring in the groceries, and then we walked around the property and took in the vista, while imbibing a glass of the local sparkling wine he had purchased along the way.

"You look great, Roz—like you're getting some sun!" Harvie said, as we settled into the Adirondacks.

"That's good to hear, considering I've barely slept for several days. It's been so crazy!"

"So tell me what's going on. I want to know what's got you so anxious."

"It's long and complicated, Harvie, but suffice it to say that every single day since I arrived here for my so-called vacation, someone has been seriously assaulted or worse—that list includes me, Molly, and McBride, by the way." I proceeded to give him a condensed version of the week's events, concluding with the alarming and very recent occurrence of Jacob's abduction.

"Holy cow, Roz."

"I've missed hearing you say that, Harvie. Anyway, that's the gist."

"That's a hell of a lot to deal with, Roz. Are you sure you're okay?"

I took his hand. "I'm not okay. I'm a mess. But I'm relieved you're here with me—and please, for tonight let's just eat and drink and you can tell me all about Montreal. Deal?"

"Deal. Let's get this barbecue fired up while there's still some daylight."

"Is there one? Oh yes, there it is. I hadn't noticed it." I really hadn't.

"It's hard to miss, Roz," he said teasing me as he lifted the cover and prepared to light it.

"It's a special skill I have," I said. "Developed over many years."

"Stay put," he said refilling my glass. "I'm just going to go inside and get the chicken soaking in a nice little marinade

I brought. We'll let it sit and absorb all that flavour and then we'll put in on the grill. While it's cooking, we can toss together a quick Caesar salad."

"Cover that chicken while it soaks, Harvie, so the cat doesn't drag it off somewhere—like onto the bed."

"Good advice. We don't need that."

I watched him disappear into the cottage and grinned. For the first time since I'd arrived in Kingsport, I felt the tension sliding away.

∽

We lit candles and ate at the table in the porch.

"How is it, Roz?"

"Melt in the mouth, Harvie. How do you do it? I've really missed you."

"My cooking, you mean?" he teased.

"That, too."

"Likewise." He took my hand. "Maybe you should move to Montreal."

"I love Montreal—but what would I do there? My French isn't good enough for work. You must do a lot of work in French."

"I manage, but it's always a challenge."

"You'll get better at it."

"I am getting better, and so would you."

"And do you like the city?"

"I'm right at home there. I've got a nice apartment in a great old Jewish neighbourhood. It's comfortable, relaxed, friendly, good food, all that. But it would be more fun if you were there."

"I'll visit," I said. "Promise. Can you hang out tomorrow for a while?"

"I need to go into Halifax early afternoon, but maybe we could both drive into Wolfville and have lunch there and then I'll head into the city."

"Let's do that. In fact we could get takeout and eat it at the botanical gardens. It must be gorgeous right now. Then, after you leave I can just go into the big lounge there and do my prep on the Beckett."

"Sounds perfect."

∽

Harvie and I were tangled up together sound asleep on my bed when the phone startled us awake. "Is that me?" I said.

"It's not me," Harvie said. "My bleep is sweeter."

"You do have a sweet bleep. What time is it?" I reached out to the bedside table and felt around for my phone. "Oh God—4 A.M."

"Yes, Roz here." I said.

"Please! I need your help! Roz, can you help me?"

I sat up. "Who is—Jacob? Is that you? Where are you?"

"Somewhere near Boston outside this garage-diner place on the highway. I got away from them when we landed in Pennsylvania."

"How on earth did you manage that?"

"I hid in this culvert under a highway exit. They had the helicopter out looking but after a while it got quiet. I've been hitching for hours—300 miles or something." His breathing was shaky, as though he was just barely holding himself together.

"I'm so relieved you're alive, Jacob. What can I do?"

"I need to get out of here—back across the border—but I have nothing. No passport, no ID, no money. If I get stopped by the cops, they'll probably throw me in jail, or worse, hand me back to those guys. I'm really scared."

"Just a minute, Jacob—don't hang up. I'm going to talk to my friend about this for a minute, okay?"

"Okay."

"Jacob is stranded on the highway near Boston—no ID, no money. He needs help. Can you suggest anything?"

"Holy cow."

"Yeah…."

"Wait—Boston! Yes…I have an old law school crony from Osgoode who went there to work at the Canadian Consulate. He's likely still there. Can Jacob get himself to the consulate?"

"Jacob? Can you hitch into Boston? My friend Harvie knows someone at the Canadian Consulate there. Who is it, Harvie?"

"Let me talk to him." Harvie took my phone. "I'll put it on speaker, Roz."

"Hi, Jacob. My name's Harvie Greenblatt. I'm a lawyer. I think I know someone who can help you, but I'll need to give him your number so you guys can make a plan together. So can I just take this number of yours from Roz's phone and give it to him?"

"Yeah—of course," Jacob said.

"Lucky thing you've got the phone."

"I know. I had it in my boot. They checked my pockets and I guess they just thought since they took me right out of the porch that I didn't have it on me."

"And is it charged?"

"Not since yesterday."

"Well, if it gets to a point where you can't use it, just head for the Canadian Consulate and ask for Gregory D'Entrement. Give him my name as a reference and hopefully I'll have talked to him by then, and he'll be expecting you."

"Okay, Canadian Consulate, Boston, Gregory D'Entrement. Is he Acadian? My Dad's a Leblanc."

"He was from New Brunswick, so yeah, I think you're right. Acadian. Jacob, listen, if I can't reach Gregory or he's

no longer there, the Canadian Consulate should have someone who can help you. I mean, I know it's not easy with no
ID. Everyone thinks everyone's a terrorist these days, but hey,
they're Canadian eh. I'm going to hand you back to Roz."

"Thanks, Mr. Greenblatt."

"Hi, Jacob. Do you think you'll be able to get a ride at this
hour?"

"It's mostly trucks out there right now. Tanker drivers usu-
ally stop."

"Really? That's funny. I'll let the RCMP know that we've
heard from you."

"No, don't! Please—if there's a leak, those guys would come
after me, for sure they would."

"You're right, Jacob. That's the last thing you need. So we'll
keep this information under wraps until we know you're safe,
which I hope will be soon. Be really careful."

"Thank you, Roz."

"Goodbye, Jacob. Good luck."

I leaned across Harvie to put my phone back on the table.

I looked into his eyes. "So—of course you knew someone
at the consulate in Boston. Amazing! Hopefully you'll be able
to reach him."

"I'll find someone to talk to—even if Gregory's not there.
We'll get the boy fixed up. I'll do it first thing."

"What'll we do in the meantime?" I said hooking my leg
over his.

"Can't think of a thing."

"It's so nice. Been awhile eh?"

'You're not kidding." Harvie pulled me closer. "Think about
it, Roz."

"I am thinking about it—that sweet bleep of yours."

He laughed. "I mean Montreal! Think about Montreal!"

Chapter 27

HARVIE WAS TALKING TO THE Canadian Consulate as soon as they opened for the day. Gregory D'Entrement was indeed still working there and they indulged in a few moments of jovial reminiscence. "No sign of him yet," Harvie said, putting his phone away. "Greg's promised to watch for Jacob and keep me in the loop."

"Why isn't he there by now?" I said, bringing the steaming Bodum and two coffee mugs to the table in the porch. "Maybe he couldn't get a ride, or maybe they caught up with him on the highway."

"Relax, Roz. It's an hour earlier in Boston. The day has just begun."

"It's not only Jacob's situation that's bothering me, Harvie. I'm distressed and angry about everything—his abduction, the murder of Aurelia Strange, the violence against McBride—all with impunity! They've pulled up stakes at Jasper Creek now and that's a kind of a victory, I guess. But it doesn't change what they did and their brazen disregard for the law. Not to mention that they were probably conducting a horrible crime against the environment every single day. There has to be something we can do, Harvie! Would you consider meeting with Arbuckle when you're in Halifax—see if the two of you can figure out some legal action here? And can't we find out once and for all whether this regional superintendent was on the take—or did he just turn a blind eye? Either way, it's not right!"

"Whoa, Roz—look at you go! You haven't even had your coffee yet."

"Well, we've been through something horrible and everybody's just so relieved they're gone. But that's not good enough."

"Okay."

"Okay, what?"

"I'll meet with Arbuckle. It's a great idea. I'll call him and arrange to see him tomorrow morning before I fly out. And I'll think about who in the public prosecutor's office might be best to take this on. I mean, it's complicated and we need someone with international experience."

"Right on, Harvie! Now you're talking!"

⟡

After our lunch in the botanical gardens in Wolfville, I stood on the sidewalk and watched Harvie's car get smaller and smaller until he reached the bottom of the hill, turned onto Main Street, and disappeared. Then I went over to the parking area, fed the meter, and grabbed my bag full of Beckett books from the back seat of Old Solid. I got a cup of chai in the environment centre, and wandered into the enormous lounge. Right by an arched window was the perfect table for me. I plunked down my books, made myself comfortable, and proceeded to stare out the window for far too long. Finally I took out my phone and called Mark. It went to message.

"Hey, Mark. When are you all arriving? I'm in Wolfville working on our stuff—wondered if you'd prefer to have dinner in town here before we head to the cottage? Or, I don't know. Call me when you get this." I set my phone to silent and put it on the table.

I randomly opened a collection of Beckett's shorter plays and found myself reading *Come and Go*—a "dramatacule" for three actresses. It was brief, maybe five minutes tops, but a perfect jewel. Beckett was a true minimalist.

"We could start with this," I said out loud. I opened my Beckett notebook.

When in doubt, make a list.

"Hello, Roz!" I looked up. It was Frida from the library, apparently just leaving the lounge. She was accompanied by another woman. "This is my co-worker, Genevieve," Frida said. "She's back."

"We finally meet!" I said, extending my hand.

"I was just telling her about the Beckett project you mentioned. I see you've got all your books there."

"Yes, we start tomorrow. So my plan is to have a reading Friday night at seven. But this is timely," I said. "Do you have a minute, Genevieve?"

"I'll go back and hold the fort," Frida said. "I know you want to ask her about the young journalist.

"Thanks, Frida," I said. Genevieve sat down, and I asked her about her work with Aurelia.

"At first I was just helping her research her ancestors" she began. "She has roots in the New England Planters who migrated to Nova Scotia from the United States around 1760. Aurelia's mother came down through the DeWolf line—as in the DeWolfs of Wolfville—that's where the name Strange comes in."

"So it's a *nom de plume*," I said, getting out a notebook.

"That's right, Aurelia chose it for her journalism work, based on her ancestor from the 1800s, T. A. Strange DeWolf. She has a genuine connection to this area. That's partly why she was so intent on finishing that article about the Bay of Fundy."

"What exactly was that article about?" I asked.

"She had discovered something illegal going on up there. She told me she was one interview away from getting confirmation of her suspicions. But she wouldn't talk about it because she was nervous that if it got around she might be in serious danger, and like all ambitious journalists, she wanted to be the one to break the story. I was supposed to meet her before I went on vacation, but she didn't show up. I was a little annoyed at the time, but now I'm just worried."

I nodded.

"After she told me about her article, I mentioned I had editing experience and she asked me if I would help her. She offered to pay me, but I said I'd be happy to look it over as a favour. So, she sent me her unedited draft. She didn't want me to read it or start working on it until she got the interview information to me. So I haven't read it myself, and I still haven't heard back."

I could hardly breathe. "Genevieve, could I see it? If I can get to the bottom of what she was investigating, we might be able to get some justice. I believe she didn't show up at your meeting because something happened to her. There may be valuable evidence right there in her material."

"Oh my God! I can forward it to you right now—do you have a smart phone?"

"BlackBerry," I said picking my phone up from the table. I gave her my address and just like magic she sent it through.

"Aurelia was intelligent and funny and deeply committed to the environment and the future of the planet," Genevieve said. "I read her article on bees and pesticides—what an indictment...very powerful. I'm relieved you're looking for her, Roz. I can't stop thinking about her."

With that, she gathered her things and rushed away.

I looked at my inbox. There it was, "Strange: Unabridged."

"I can't go on. I'll go on…." I said, quoting Beckett. I dove into the "Strange" file.

"You Wouldn't Want to Drink It" by A. Strange

It was a dark day when I learned my friend was dating a man who broke the law twice a week, every week. The crime involved my favorite place in the world—the Bay of Fundy in Nova Scotia. If you haven't seen it, you should plan to go there immediately. It's not a tourist trap; much of it is isolated—it's just you and the highest tides in the world.

We've gotten into a serious mess here in the northeastern U.S. Much of our prime arable land is scarred with fracking wells. Hydraulic Fracturing: releasing gas from shale rock. Often the shale rock is deep underground. Vital to the fracking process is fresh potable water with added chemicals: benzene, methanol, formaldehyde, toluene, xylene, monoethanolamine, and ammonium bi-sulphite to name a few of the 22 commonly used. These chemicals are carcinogens, mutagens, neurotoxins, and endocrine disruptors. Each fracking wellhead requires 3.5 million gallons of water per frack.

The chemically infused water is pumped into the wells until the pressure breaks up the shale and releases the gas. There are so many wells that America now has more gas than it needs. Once those millions of gallons of chemically enhanced potable water crack open that shale, the water returns to the surface as 'Fracking Wastewater' or 'Flowback' as the industry calls it. When it comes back up, it's laden with even more poisons from the gas itself.

And what can be done with all this poisoned water? Surface evaporating ponds take up acres and acres of land. The ponds often breach the barriers and contaminated fluid pours out, poisons the land, and leaks into the groundwater. The contamination is so serious, some farmers in Pennsylvania can set their tap water on fire. Some of this wastewater is being stored in deep well injection sites in Ohio. But, it's an expensive process, and many sites are now full to bursting. The path of least resistance is to wait until dark, and dump it into a stream or a river. If caught, pay the fines! And chalk it up to the cost of doing business—it's cheaper than any other solution.

One recent summer, a gas company's head honcho was vacationing in eastern Canada. He became intrigued by the natural openings that lead into large caverns inside the basaltic rock that formed Nova Scotia's North Mountain on the Bay of Fundy 200 million years ago.

Those caverns are called 'vaults.' They often reach from just under the surface to deep down below sea level and extend out into the Bay of Fundy, finally opening into the ocean far from shore.

A telecom company had built and then abandoned an industrial bridge and a road that led up to a ridge where one of the natural vaults happened to be. It was marked on the map "Jasper Creek Vault." The telecom company welcomed the money it was offered for use of the bridge and the road.

The gas company's head honcho was never just on vacation; he always had his thinking cap on, and he could envision hundreds of tankers delivering that flowback water up to that forested ridge and releasing it neatly into the vault. Through the vault, the water would find its way into the Bay of Fundy. These are the highest tides in the world, and every day, twice a day, that wastewater would be carried away on the tides and be so diluted, it would be as though it never happened.

The following summer he conducted a secret test with two tankers full of wastewater. He arranged for them to drive up to the vault and release 20,000 gallons of toxic water. It completely disappeared—his experiment worked! Next, he custom-made hardware to protect the vault surface and to efficiently attach the tankers' hoses to a receiving pipe he placed in the vault's opening.

He had ancestral roots in Nova Scotia and over the years he'd made good friends. So once he decided to go forward, he set about making quiet arrangements in this isolated part of the province.

Back home in America, he hired lots of eager out-of-work truckers and organized a secret route so they could cross the border from a farm in Maine to New Brunswick, and enter Canada with no fuss or muss. He had really authentic-looking Nova Scotia license plates made and when everything was in place, he travelled through the northeastern United States and organized the pick-up of thousands of gallons of dirty flowback water that was being kept in evaporation ponds or sitting in holding tanks on the countless shale gas fields.

Gas producers were relieved to pay him well to eliminate that wastewater problem. It remedied a big headache—and they didn't ask any questions. It was like a secret adventure, and everyone involved felt like they were helping to clean up America. The truckers were making a good living and there was no end to it—there was always more and more fracking wastewater. The CEO became a kind of hero.

It's a fluke that I learned about this secret activity, starting with my friend's boyfriend who was hired as a trucker. But I did learn it, and now that I'm carrying the burden of knowledge it feels like the heaviest thing in the world, so it's time to crack it open for everyone to see. I hear the siren call of the mermaids and I'm on the side of the Bay of Fundy.

I won't name the truckers until last. I'm starting with the executive and his company, and then I'm going to track down the names of all the "on the take" people on both sides of the border: the gas companies in America who are participating, and the bureaucrats and others who are in the know in Kings County and getting a little something for their silence.

Here comes the first name. I'm just about to have an interview with the head honcho himself, Steven Wynne Ratchford of Harness Energy, a Pennsylvania-registered company. Ironically, he and I are related. We share an ancestor, Hannah, a Ratchford who married into the DeWolfs back in 1800. I told him this and he said since we're long-lost cousins, the interview should take place over dinner.

We're eating at The Tempest, and I'm hoping for the Catch of the Day!

I called Riley immediately and filled her in on the Jacob situation. "So now we're waiting," I said, "and Riley, there's something else I've just learned."

"Where are you, Roz?"

"I'm in Wolfville—at the Irving Centre."

Five minutes later, I was on my way down Main Street to the detachment.

∽

I sat down across from Riley. "I just got a draft of Aurelia's very informative article from a librarian she was confiding in," I said, forwarding it to her. "You should have it now."

Riley's phone rang. "It's your friend Arbuckle," she said. "Hello, Detective Arbuckle. Roz has just arrived at my office. Shall I put you on speakerphone?" She nodded at me. "Here we go," she said.

"Hi, Roz," he said. "Listen—I had a little chat with Harvie today and things are moving along in Boston with that boy, Jacob."

"What's happening?" I said.

"Well, the consulate needs an envoy to come down there, vouch for him, and accompany him back to Canada. It's got to be someone official, so it can't be you, or a family member. I was thinking you could do that, Corporal Monaghan."

"Riley's a perfect choice, Donald," I said jumping in. "She knows Jacob and she's up to speed with the latest developments in this Jasper Creek situation too. But Donald, would this decision involve Superintendant Dudgeon?"

"I can set this up on this end as an official secondment. What do you think, Corporal Monaghan?"

"If you arrange it, I can go immediately," Riley said.

"So, he's okay then—Jacob?" I said.

"Apparently he was rattled and hungry when he finally arrived there, but they're putting him up inside the consulate while we sort this out, so he's safe. It was lucky that Harvie gave them the head's up, or who knows, he might have been turned away. I mean, let's face it, it's a pretty wild story."

"It's a pretty wild state of affairs," I said. "I know much more now. I've come to Riley's office to bring her an article that Aurelia drafted just before she met her demise. She describes in detail the activity that was going on up at Jasper Creek, and names the American CEO who set it up. She talks about how she was planning to interview him over a meal in Wolfville. Shall I send it to you?"

"Absolutely. Send it now. This is very timely. Harvie and I are planning to meet tomorrow morning before he leaves."

"I'd like to be there too, but I'll be busy falling down a deep well."

"What well is that?"

"The Samuel Beckett well, with a group of wacky, brilliant performers who are coming up to Kingsport tonight."

"That's right—your other life," Arbuckle said. "Corporal Monaghan, I'll be back to you with your travel itinerary. I'll work on getting this organized ASAP."

⁓

I left the detachment and headed back to the environmental centre to continue the Beckett prep. My phone buzzed. It was Mark.

"Hey, Roz. Everything as planned except Regan can't join us until tomorrow morning—she's finishing a grant application."

"Of course she is."

"Yup—another one. Deadline's midnight tonight. Otherwise, we're all good. Oh, except Cym finally broke up with her girlfriend."

"You mean today?"

"Well, it's been coming for a while…but, yeah, today."

"Is she okay…I mean is she focused?"

"Oh, she'll be fine. This will be good for her, throwing herself into the work. So anyway, Ellie, Cym, and I could meet you at a restaurant, or we can just come out to the cottage and make something there—whatever you like."

"You know what, I'm probably only good for a couple more hours of reading. My life has been a tad too crazy. So why don't you come straight to the cottage."

"Don't worry about dinner—we'll pick something up."

"Mark! That's two meals in a row for me!"

"So life is good?"

"Yeah, except for all the bad stuff."

"You're funny. See you soon—probably no later than seven. We're all really grooving on Beckett, Roz—all Beckett all the time."

ॐ

By the time I left to go back to Kingsport, I had actually managed to draft a plan of which pieces I thought would feature their skills and make a compelling presentation, including which order might work best, considering casting, bits of costume, and how the overall reading would build emotionally. At least I'm prepared to start the work tomorrow, I thought. Who knows where we'll end up?

"Company's coming," I said to the cat as I hastily tidied up the place and checked that there were enough beds made up to accommodate everyone.

I glanced out the window. Speak of the little devils! The actors' van was rolling down Longspell Road towards the cottage. I dashed out through the porch and along the driveway to greet them as they pulled in.

"Now what would Beckett say?" I called, as they climbed out of the van.

Cym turned in a circle looking around. "Beckett would say, 'A country road. A tree. Evening.'" I recognized it as the opening setting from *Waiting for Godot*.

Mark jumped in. "He would say, 'All the dead voices. They make a noise like wings.'"

Ellie continued, "'They make a noise like feathers.'"

And Cym, "'Like leaves.'"

And finally all of us together: "'Like ashes.'"

"Good on ya," I said, trying to hug them all at the same time. "You *are* in the groove!"

"I was just reading that section out loud in the car," Ellie said. "It's so ghosty."

"I know," I said. "Wait until we look at *Footfalls*—I finally figured that one out today. It's really ghosty. We can work on it in the morning!"

"But first, let's make food!" Mark said. "I'm starving."

"What did you bring?"

"I'm making burgers. You have a barbecue, right?"

"Of course," I said. "Right over there by the porch steps."

"I'll do the salad," Ellie said.

"And I'll open the wine…right now," Cym said. "I'll bring you a glass, Roz."

The girls disappeared into the house, while Mark lit the grill.

I dropped into the Adirondack.

"Great!" I said. "Looks like you guys have got this."

Chapter 28

OUR FIRST DAY OF WORK in the arts centre studio was painstaking but exhilarating. Regan called early to say she wouldn't be able to join us until noon, but we jumped right in, looking at *Footfalls*, a short play, only five pages long.

"So the cast is two women," I said. "One of them, May, is visible. The other, Voice, is offstage, as though in another room, or another world. We'll just start with this image of May horizontally pacing back and forth across the stage. Let's all try it to see what it feels like…one two three four five six seven, wheel, and back the other way four five six seven, wheel." The actors continued the pacing and began to find the rhythm. "Voice says, 'Watch how feat she wheels.'"

"Is feat a pun on feet?" Ellie asked.

"It makes us think of feet," I said, "but it also makes us realize how well-practiced she is—like she's been doing it forever. Later, Voice tells us that May had the carpet removed, saying, 'I must hear the feet, however faint they fall.'"

We went through the first section, with Cym reading May and Ellie reading Voice.

"Let's look at the next section," I said, "which May calls 'Sequel.' This is where the ghost story emerges more clearly. Let's see if we can break it down."

"This is my favourite part from Sequel, Roz," Cym said. "May is speaking, and I'm going to read all the stage directions that Beckett puts in too."

"Go for it," I said, impressed that she had studied it.

She began: "'The semblance. (Faint, though by no means invisible, in a certain light.) (Pause.) Grey rather than white, a pale shade of grey. (Pause.) Tattered. (Pause.) A tangle of tatters. (Pause.) A faint tangle of pale grey tatters.'"

Cym stopped and looked us. "I mean, 'a faint tangle of pale grey tatters'—she's a ghost!" She continued reading. "'(Pause.) Watch it pass—(pause)—watch her pass –before the candelabrum, how its flames, their light….like moon through passing rack.'"

"That's ghosty," Mark said. "First he says, 'watch it pass,' and then corrects to 'her'."

"And that line—'like moon through passing rack.' What is 'passing rack'?" Ellie asked.

I was prepared. "'Rack' is an obscure word for a mass of clouds driven before a wind in the upper air. So with that phrase, Beckett is likening the apparition's pale grey tattered image as she passes in front of the candelabra to clouds as they obscure and reveal the moon." I looked at my notes. "One of the definitions of 'semblance' is 'apparition,'" I said. "Or 'an appearance or outward seeming of something which is not actually there.'"

Mark said, "There are other clues in the text that she's an apparition, like 'slipping through the locked door,' and 'vanishing the way she came.'"

"You're right, this is spooky!" Ellie said. "In fact, I'm getting all creeped out!"

"I'm actually loving this ghost idea as a theme for which pieces we choose," I said. "Let's see what else we can find."

"We could call it 'Ghosty Bits from Beckett,'" Cym said.

"Can we look at *That Time*?" Mark said.

"You're tuned in, Mark," I said. "Beckett wrote *That Time* in '76—the same year he wrote *Footfalls*. He wrote them both for the Royal Court Theatre's celebration of his seventieth birthday."

"Listen to this from *That Time*." Mark began to read: "'Not a living soul in the place only yourself and the odd attendant drowsing around in his felt shufflers not a sound to be heard only every now and then a shuffle of felt drawing near then dying away.'"

"They're the footfalls of the attendant," Cym said.

"Yes! Great connection," I said.

Suddenly the sun broke into the room, startling us as the door opened. It was Corporal Monaghan poking her head in.

"Riley! Have you got a hankering to read some Beckett?"

"Sorry to interrupt, Roz. I just need a minute."

Riley and I left the room and went into the hallway. Through the closed door, I could hear Cym say, "Wow—who was that? Is she single?"

"Let's step outside," I said. We went into the yard and wandered over towards the barn.

"The medical examiner's gotten back to me, Roz. Aurelia was in fact poisoned. An overdose of the date rape drug GHB killed her. It's an anesthetic—and you have to be really careful with it."

"So that story Jacob told us about her being dragged like a rag doll into the SUV makes sense," I said.

Riley nodded. "And, there was no water in her lungs so she was dead before she was in the bay."

"Awful," I said.

"I know. Detective Arbuckle's on his way here to interview the manager and waiters at the restaurant this afternoon to see if anybody remembers anything. I'm going to join him there."

"I'm with you in spirit," I said. "Let me know if you find anything out."

"Tonight Arbuckle and I are heading to the airport to fly to the States. The information from Aurelia's article should help him track down the CEO of Harness Energy, and he wants to start investigating all that stuff right away."

"He doesn't waste a minute. So you're going to Boston and he's going to Pennsylvania?"

"I'm going to Boston—that's all I know at this point."

A car was coming down the long driveway. It was Regan arriving from the city.

"Our missing actor has arrived," I said.

"I'll be in touch," Riley said, as she got into the cruiser.

Regan was parking and I went over to welcome her and bring her into the rehearsal room.

After greetings, hugs, and Regan's rant about the horrors of grant writing, we told her about our ghost theme idea.

"That fits with Beckett's *Play* too," Regan said. "I mean, three people in urns…they're definitely ghosts."

"Yes," I said, "and condemned to going over and over the same infidelity forever."

"Although, that is kind of what people do in life…" Cym said.

"You would know," Mark said.

"Okay, you guys," I said. "Save it for later."

Ellie said, "What about *Rockabye*? The ghosty rocker that won't stop rocking—'Dead one night, in the rocker, in her best black, head fallen,…rocking away….'"

"But the theme and tone of those pieces is very different from *Catastrophe*, don't you think?" Regan countered. "I mean, *Catastrophe* is stylized, but very much in our world today. A world where torture happens. How do we bring all that together with the ghost theme?"

"Well, a theme is not a rule, and at this stage we're exploring," I reminded them. "It's tempting to include *Catastrophe*."

"We have to," Mark said. "I really want to do it."

"Well then—why not?" I said. "It will be interesting for us to see how it goes."

∽

By the end of that first day our brains were addled from trying to absorb so many Beckett pieces.

"Okay, tomorrow morning we'll just shake it down and choose, and then work like crazy on them," I said, wrapping up. "We'll start with *Come and Go* first thing. I mean, it's perfect for you three." I looked at the women, who responded by grabbing each other's hands and reciting the final line together: "I can feel the rings."

"So bring your old-lady hats, and we'll dig around here and hopefully find a bench," I said.

"I brought a bench. It's in the van," Mark said. "So are the hats." We all looked at him. "Can't help it, girls. I'm psychic."

"Also," I said, "a reminder that I've asked Sophie to read the final section of *Eh Joe* in the presentation, so we'll figure out how that fits into the order of things."

We bumped into Heather on our way out. I introduced her, and asked if we could invite the company of actors who had just arrived and were rehearsing for the centre's summer show. She said she would spread the word. "Friday at seven!" I said.

"I'll definitely be there," said Heather.

"Come on, guys," Mark said, "let's unpack the rest of the stuff, so it will all be in the room if we need it tomorrow."

As the company followed Mark out, Heather said, "So you remember Jacob who works with us part-time…did you hear about him being abducted from his house?"

I nodded.

"I'm really worried about him," she said.

"Me too."

∽

The next day, we continued the work and settled on an order by dinnertime. After working through *Catastrophe*, we decided to include it. I'd brought the chopping block from the cottage to serve as the plinth that The Protagonist stands on. And Mark produced an enormous prop cigar for The Director's role, being read in drag by Regan sporting a large moustache. We set up the space with a couple of folding black flats on either side of the playing area to create wings. The troupe organized all their props and various costume and set pieces to whichever side would keep the action flowing.

"This is the problem with minimalism," I said, looking at everything. "Too much stuff!"

∽

Friday morning was upon us. The actors headed into Canning to get breakfast at Al's Diner and I was eating my oatmeal and talking to the cat when McBride and Sophie arrived at the cottage.

"I wasn't expecting you until this afternoon," I said to Sophie.

She gestured towards McBride. "He's been commandeered," she said, and went out to get her things from Ruby Sube.

"For what?" I said to McBride.

"I'm off to Kentville, doing a little digging into the recent activities of Regional Superintendent Dudgeon."

I looked at him. "So…there's been a development?"

"According to Arbuckle, one of the wait staff at The Tempest remembered the three of them, and recognized a photo of Dudgeon."

"So Arbuckle contacted you?"

"He called me Wednesday night from the airport, asked if I'd follow up. I made an appointment with Dudgeon's secretary to meet with him later today. I was planning to drive Sophie up here anyway."

"Be careful, McBride. You know that if you corner him, anything could happen."

"You think?" he said, grinning. "I'll see you tonight—7 P.M.!"

Sophie travelled with me to rehearsal.

"McBride looks great!" I said to her.

"Fast recovery eh? He's way better…and he was happy to get that call from Arbuckle. He's champing at the bit!" She looked at me. "Don't worry, Roz, he'll be careful."

We arrived at the centre. The actors' van pulled in beside us, and we all got out. They welcomed Sophie, and we stood for a moment in the sun and took some deep breaths.

"Ready to work?" I said to them all.

"You bet!"

"Here we go. Let's put it together."

Chapter 29

PEOPLE CAME TO THE READING. Björn and Grace arrived early, and took a stroll through the fields, Björn stooping over every now and again to pick up a rock. Jeffrey was a surprise. I knew his wife was away visiting their daughter in New Brunswick so he was on his own. I was relieved that he didn't show up with George. Frida and Genevieve arrived. I greeted them warmly. In the circumstances, I couldn't tell Genevieve what we now knew about Aurelia, but explained that much had transpired and assured her I would soon come to the library to fill her in. I told Frida I would be returning the book Aurelia had borrowed.

The actors and designers from the resident company burbled in, and the three rows of seats quickly began to fill.

"I'm nervous," I said to Heather. "And it's just a reading."

"Yeah, but it's never just a reading is it? We're always on the line—and isn't that exactly where we want to be?"

"You're right," I said. "On the line. That's exactly where we want to be."

A couple of minutes after seven, when everyone was settled, I went up front to welcome the crowd. I was just about to speak when McBride slipped in and grabbed a seat at the end of the row, nearest the door.

"Okay. Hello…welcome! We're thrilled you're all here. We're at the beginning of an exploration of Samuel Beckett's short works, which the company hopes to tour this fall. This is a reading of eight short pieces. We have minimal lights, actors holding books, carrying the odd chair on and off—you know the drill."

There were murmurs of recognition from the theatre crowd. "There'll be no intermission and it's just a little over an hour. We'd prefer you to hold applause between pieces and allow the whole thing to flow as one. Let's see…oh, right—we brought refreshments! So if you can stay afterwards, please join us across the hall in the art gallery. We'd like that."

At that moment the door pushed open a crack. We could hear whispering from the hallway, but no one came in. "Tell whoever it is that they're welcome," I said to Heather. "It's not too late. It's fine."

Heather went over and opened the door. She gasped and put her hand to her mouth. We all stared as Jacob entered the room, accompanied by Corporal Monaghan, Donald Arbuckle, Jacob's mother, and his sister.

"Thank heavens!" Heather said, reaching out to give Jacob a hug. Various people in the audience who knew Jacob from the centre nodded and gave him the thumbs up and things got a bit chaotic and chatty as they found seats. Riley and Arbuckle came over to me. "Sorry for the disruption, Roz," Riley said. "Didn't want to miss this. We'll fill you in afterwards."

"I can't believe you're here!" I said. "Make yourselves comfortable. We're just getting ready to start."

I looked at Arbuckle. "So you decided to check out my other life?"

"I'm thinking about a career change," he said with a wry grin.

He and Riley took a couple of seats at the end of the second row. Jacob sat in front of them with Heather, and everyone got quiet again. "Great," I said. "Now, we really are all here."

The playing area had been pre-set for the first piece with a simple bench, centre. The three girls had memorized their lines for *Come and Go* to get things off to a good start.

"Just for the beginning of the show," I said to the audience, "close your eyes and imagine the lights going to black. I'll say 'okay' when its time to open them." The audience, as one, closed their eyes.

Flo, Vi, and Ru, the three old ladies in their big hats, came out from the wings and got quickly into position on the bench, while I went and took a seat in the first row.

"Okay," I said softly to the audience.

The audience collectively opened their eyes, and the evening began with Ru's line "When did we three last meet?" The pieces flew by—each like a strange jewel with its own particular light. After *Footfalls*, Sophie entered, placed her chair, and began to read the last section of *Eh Joe*. Her voice was so intimate, the audience was mesmerized. Soon she came to the final phrases:

> "Lies down in the end with her face a few feet from the tide…clawing at the shingle now…Finishes the pills… there's love for you…Eh Joe? Scoops a little cup for her face in the stones…the green one…The narrow one…always pale…the pale eyes…The look they shed before… The way they opened after…Spirit made light."

Then, as Sophie exited, the exquisite strains of Schubert's "Nacht und Traume" sung by Dietrich Fischer-Dieskau filled the space, underscoring the final piece—a remarkably simple dream of solace—and then "fade to silence." It was over.

There was a moment of profound stillness and then the audience burst into applause and wouldn't stop clapping.

When we talked about it later, we were pretty certain that Beckett's warm ghosty spirit had been right there in the room with us.

The audience and actors crowded into the art gallery for refreshments, but Jacob remained in his seat. Arbuckle and Riley were there just behind him. Sophie was at the other end of the row talking to McBride.

I went straight to Jacob. "So no problems crossing the border?" I said.

"Not in the company of Corporal Monaghan," he said, glancing back at her. "It all went smooth, though I'm pretty sure most of the passengers thought I was a convict."

"I see. And how are you?"

"Truth is, I was doing okay…until Sophie read. I guess it just…cut a little too close to home."

Then, just like that, he began to sob.

As I watched him, I had an alarming vision.

I could see what had really happened.

Why the death-image that Sophie presented had brought it all back for him.

"Jacob…it was you who tied Aurelia into the tree, wasn't it?" I said.

Arbuckle and Riley had become quiet.

Jacob looked at me. "I did find her in the cave, but it was too late. I tried to revive her—but she was gone." He looked directly at me. "Her eyes were open—but she was gone. That tree was just there on the beach, right outside that cave, like it was waiting for her. One of the drivers had given me an American flag, and I climbed up through the undergrowth to my house and got it. I took some rope and put it in my boat and dragged it across the beach to the cave.

"After I wrapped her in the flag, I carried her out and placed her body on the trunk and tied her arms into the tree roots. By then the moon was rising and the tide was flowing…. I rowed out, pulling the tree to the other side of Cape Split. Then I let her go…. I didn't want her to just disappear. I wanted someone along the coast to find her—to see what they'd done to her."

"I saw her, Jacob," I said. "Early the next morning—I'm the one who called it in, but they swooped in and took her away before anyone noticed."

Riley reached down and put her hand on Jacob's shoulder. "It's okay," she said.

Jacob looked back at her. "I was so afraid the truth wouldn't come out," he said.

"Well it's out now," Arbuckle said, "and who knows, if you hadn't done that and Roz hadn't seen her, that bunch might still be up there emptying one tanker after another of poisoned water the ocean. But that's over now."

"Is it?" I said to Arbuckle.

"We've got Harvie working on the international front, Roz, and true to form, he's moving fast. I went straight to the Environmental Protection Agency when I was down there, and we discussed the possibility of offering the tanker drivers leniency if they're willing to testify about their part in Ratchford's scheme. We'll see. They're considering it. If the drivers come forward, it would save a lot of money on the litigation side. Harvie's already got one of the lawyers in your office working on the case, and you'll be researching the ins and outs of the international extradition treaty as soon as you're back at work. Monday, right?"

"I'm all over it, Donald," I said. "And dare I ask what happened with Dudgeon?"

Arbuckle grinned. "McBride cornered Dudgeon today like no one else can. Got him to admit he was turning a blind eye to illegal dumping into the Bay of Fundy. And Aurelia knew it. She must have been one fearless girl. When Riley and I went to the restaurant, they remembered them. Apparently, she accused Dudgeon—actually made a bit of a scene. He played it cool, though, got up from the table and went to the bar to buy them all drinks, wanted her to calm down and talk about it. It's possible that's when he slipped the GHB into her glass, which, according to the medical examiner, is unquestionably what killed her."

"Did McBride ask him?"

"Total denial. We've also secured the bluff—all the hardware that's built around the vault, clear evidence of how the dumping was carried out. So I'm sitting here with a list of charges as long as my arm!"

"What about Aurelia?" I looked at Riley.

"The medical examiner is releasing her and we've been in touch with her family. We'll be sending her body to Portland on Monday," Riley said.

People had begun to drift in from the reception to look for us and say good night.

Björn came over. "All the pieces were wonderful, Roz, and many I had never seen, nothing like a good dose of Beckett."

He greeted Jacob warmly. "You've had quite a number of adventures these past few days. It's good to see you, my friend."

Then Katie was there, squeezing between us all to sit beside Jacob.

"Hi, Katie," I said. "You remember me?"

"You're Roz. I remember. Jacob said you're the one that put this whole show together."

"We all worked on it. I'm kind of the outside eye."

"Well, you did an awesome job."

"Thank you—that means a lot to me," I said. "I'm glad you made it."

"I'm never letting my brother out of my sight again!" She hugged Jacob.

Jacob grinned at her, and messed up her hair.

"Hey!" she said. "Stop that!"

Mark hurried in from outside, a little out of breath. "We're all packed up, Roz—getting ready to hit the road. We've got a gig tomorrow."

I stood and nodded at Mark.

"You okay?" I asked Jacob.

"Getting there," he said.

I followed Mark out to the van where everyone was lingering in the warm summer air.

"Okay," I said. "I think we're on for a fall tour, don't you? You all did great work tonight!"

"More Beckett!" Ellie said. "I love that stuff!"

"We're just getting started," I said. "I'll see you all in the city next week."

Then Sophie was beside me saying farewell to the company and giving everyone a hug. We waved as Regan's car and the company van made their way up the familiar driveway.

"You and McBride are coming to Kingsport for the night, right?" I said to Sophie.

"Yup," she said. "Molly's there, waiting for us. McBride didn't tell you?"

"I'm sure the cat has held her own," I said. "Gorgeous reading tonight, Soph."

"Thanks for including me, Roz. It was really a powerful event. What a great audience!"

McBride came out of the building and stood with us in the balmy air.

"We should all do something tomorrow," I said. "Last two days for me."

"We could have a picnic," Sophie said.

"On the Bay of Fundy," McBride said with a grin.

At that moment, Darlene and Katie came out of the centre with Jacob and the three of us watched the family make its way over to the parking lot. "That was a lovely show, dear," Darlene called over. "You can come by the cafeteria for beef with barley soup anytime."

"Thank you, Darlene. I might take you up on that."

I looked at McBride. "You were too busy sleeping to try her excellent soup," I teased.

Just then, Riley appeared with Arbuckle.

"So I haven't even had a chance to ask you about Boston," I said to her.

They were both silent.

"Something's wrong," I said.

"I just got an email," Riley said.

"It changes the water on the beans," Arbuckle added.

Riley, seeing that Jacob was about to pull out of the parking lot, suddenly bolted away from us. "Strike while the iron is hot," she shouted back to me.

"Can we take Jacob into the studio here, and sit down with him?" Arbuckle asked me.

"Sure," I said, "we have it booked until eleven."

"You two join us," he said to McBride and Sophie. "I'll tell Jacob's mother to take Katie and go home." Arbuckle crossed to the driveway, where Riley had stopped them.

"Let's' go in and set up some chairs," I said.

Chapter 30

"It's about Aurelia's car, Jacob," Arbuckle said, once we were all seated around a work table in the studio. "The one you said you were driving that night. Corporal Monaghan has just received the results from the forensic lab and there's residue of vomit and GHB in the car. So tell us what really happened."

Jacob shook his head. "I don't understand what you're saying."

Riley cut in. "Jacob, the story you told Roz and me when we found you up on the ridge, about how Aurelia was dragged out of Steve's rental and then driven down to Caroline Beach in the SUV, is now looking like a complete fabrication. If you were in her car waiting up the road from the restaurant, maybe you did pick her up. Did you?"

He was staring at the floor.

"Tell the truth, Jacob," I said.

There was a long silence. Then he looked up. "I watched the three of them come out of the restaurant. She told me they offered her a drive, but she refused. She said she had a car. After they drove away, she took out her phone to call me, but I pulled up to the curb and she got in beside me. I remember she said, 'You got my car fixed!' and I said, 'Surprise.'"

"So they didn't know you were there?" Arbuckle said.

"They were gone, and I'd made sure they didn't see me."

"And then?"

"Then, I was driving her home, up to the cabin. I asked her how it went. I mean, I had a right to know."

"Of course! Because you were Aurelia's source, weren't you? Her informant," I said.

"When she first moved up to the cabin, she told me why she'd come here, what she was investigating. She was so into it—I wanted to help her. So I went down there to Jasper Creek and asked for a job. They hired me part-time. I helped out with everything. I got to know a lot of the drivers, I found out who the boss was. I chauffeured people, I picked people up at the airport. I kept my head down and learned everything I could about the whole scheme and in the evenings I would pass it all on to Aurelia." He paused. "I was her secret partner—that's what she called me. So yeah—I wanted to know what she'd told them and how they reacted. I was worried about her doing the interview. But she was determined to get some real quotes from Ratchford. She didn't expect that cop to be there. She thought Ratchford would be alone."

"So what did she tell you about the meeting?" I said.

"She said after she told them she was an environmental journalist and what she was working on, they argued with her and said it was a perfectly safe disposal method and that lots of people were getting work and it would be best for everyone if she just forgot about it. She told them she could list all the dangerous substances that are in fracking waste-water and that the citizens of Nova Scotia deserve to know exactly what was being pumped into the Bay of Fundy. She said she asked the cop point-blank how he could turn a blind eye and suggested that maybe he was on the take and then he told her to calm down, that he would never be in-volved with anything that wasn't safe. And she said, 'So you admit you're involved!' He said that they could work this out, that they should all have a nice dinner, and then he went over to the bar to get the three of them drinks."

Riley leaned towards Arbuckle. "Dudgeon would have access to GHB," she said. "There've been several seizures of the stuff. There was a rash of it at the university this spring."

"That could explain why he was there," McBride said. "To see what she was up to and shut her up if need be."

"Premeditated," Arbuckle said.

"Do you think she told them about her connection with you, Jacob?" I asked him. "About you providing her with information?"

"She wouldn't do that," he said.

"But if she did, that might be why they abducted you."

"They probably figured I'd learned too much just working there."

"Hold on—let's not get sidetracked. So, you're driving her home," Arbuckle said. "Then what happened?"

"She was so hyper, she said she had a couple of good quotes; she was really jazzed about exposing the scheme. She couldn't wait to start writing. It was like she was on a high. We were already up on the mountain when she suddenly felt really sick. She was as white as a sheet. Then she said, 'Oh my God, Jacob, I think they've poisoned me!' So I said, 'I'm taking you down to the hospital!' But she was panicking. She was crying and convulsing and throwing up—she was trying to open the car door. So I pulled over and went to help her out of the car. She was just retching and then she fell down on the road. It was horrible. I was sitting on the road with her...and she just...she died.

"I didn't know what to do. I put her in the car and took her down to Caroline Beach. I was going to put her in the cave, but that tree was there—and when I saw it I decided to send her out on the tide so she'd be found and—you know the rest...."

"We don't know everything, Jacob," Arbuckle said. "For instance, why did you clean the car?"

"It reeked. I washed it out. Then I took it home and parked it in our garage." He shook his head. "I was so scared. I told my mother I'd taken her to Kentville to get the shuttle to the airport."

"That's true," I said. "Darlene told me that in the cafeteria. But Jacob, if Aurelia was never in the cave, why did I find part of her name written on the rock with her own lipstick?" I asked.

"That morning you found me coming out of the cave, I'd put the letters there, and I left the lipstick tube on the ground. I wanted whoever found McBride to know the same people had hurt her." He looked at me. "What are you going to do?"

"We're building a case, Jacob," I said. "Against Ratchford. Against Dudgeon. The two thugs."

"And you, my friend, are part of that case," Arbuckle said.

"I wouldn't hurt her. I would have done anything for her. I loved her."

"If nothing else, you're a key witness, so you're not going anywhere," Arbuckle said.

"I want to help. I'll do whatever you need me to do."

"Good," Arbuckle said. "We'll release you on your own recognizance and we'll expect you to be available for further questioning whenever we need you."

"Are we done for now?" Riley asked.

Arbuckle nodded.

"I'll take you home Jacob," she said. "Let's go."

I walked them out. Jacob got into the cruiser. I asked Riley if she thought taking him home was the right thing to do.

"I got to know him pretty well this past couple of days," she said. "He's been through a rough time. I think he's a good kid, and he's smart. In fact, he says he wants to join the RCMP. And you know what, if he gets through all this, I think he'll make a good cop."

∽

An hour later McBride and Sophie and I sat around the porch table in my cottage finishing the takeout ribs and salad we'd picked up on the way home. The animals were fed and everything was calm.

I told them what Riley had said about Jacob wanting to join the RCMP.

"What do you think, Roz? Do you buy Jacob's story?" McBride asked.

"I definitely believe he was Aurelia's source, and that he wanted to help her uncover the truth. But he got in too deep, doing errands for those creeps, practically running the place some days. Things got crazy."

Sophie said, "I believe him. And he went through something horrific in that car with her that night. Those are the symptoms of a GHB overdose—the euphoria, the compulsive talking, the vomiting. I experienced it once—a long time ago. I didn't get the convulsions and of course I didn't die, but that is what happens, and it can happen fast. When she died, it makes sense that he panicked."

"If it was Jacob who poisoned her," I said, "why would he have wanted to float the body through the channel for everyone to see?"

"Jacob didn't have the motive to harm her that those guys had," McBride said. "I think they wanted to put a good scare into her to shut her up, and they ended up killing her with the stuff. That's why Dudgeon was so rattled and defensive when I paid him a visit."

"They must have done it," I said. "Otherwise, why would they go so far as to remove her from the basin in a helicopter and bury her up on the ridge? They were trying to get rid of the evidence."

"They botch things up, don't they? Look what happened when they tried to kill you, McBride. They blew it," Sophie said, teasing him.

"I'm too tough," he said, taking her hand.

I stood, and started to gather our dishes up and put things away. "So yeah, McBride," I said. "In answer to your question, I do believe him."

"So much happened today," Sophie said. "The reading feels like it was a week ago."

"Maybe you can join the Beckett tour in the fall," I said, "if you're not shooting that crime series."

"I didn't tell you, Roz—I got the gig!"

"Really? Congrats, Sophie! So you'll be going to Toronto in August."

Sophie nodded.

"And will you have company?" I said, nodding towards McBride.

"I'm working on him," she said, grinning.

"We'll see," said McBride.

"What's the part?" I asked her.

"I'm playing an investigator…. I've been studying your every move."

I laughed. "I can't wait to see your interpretation of me on TV."

"You'll have to come and visit me," Sophie said. "I'll have lots of room—apparently they're renting me an apartment."

"Maybe I will, Soph. Take the long weekend in September before rehearsals start. Visit you, and then drop into Montreal on the way back…."

∽

The next morning Sophie and McBride and Molly left early for Halifax, and the cat and I slept in. When I got up, I made myself a cup of tea, grabbed an intriguing mystery from the cottage bookshelf, and stepped out into the yard.

It was sunny and fragrant and there was no wind. With some trepidation, I looked out across the basin. The tide was coming in, and for the first time I wasn't overwhelmed by images of Aurelia. I hoped she was now at peace. That we would attain the justice she so bravely sought.

I breathed deep and settled into the Adirondack. The cat jumped up onto the flat wooden arm and purred. "Happy days," I said, scratching her ears.

LINDA MOORE RESIDES IN HALIFAX and has a cottage in Kingsport, Nova Scotia, on the Minas Basin. She works as a theatre director across Canada and was artistic director of Neptune Theatre in Halifax throughout the nineties. She has received several Robert Merritt Awards, including the 2015 award for Outstanding Direction. Linda has been a guest director at McGill, Memorial, UVic, and Dalhousie and was the Crake Fellow in Drama at Mount Allison. She is the recipient of an Honorary Doctor of Letters from Saint Mary's University. *The Fundy Vault* is her second novel in the Rosalind Mystery series.

More Mysterious Reads from Vagrant Press

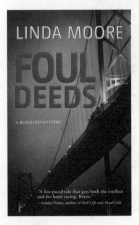

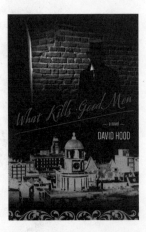

Foul Deeds
Linda Moore

978-155109-946-0

What Kills Good Men
David Hood

978-177108-350-8

Disposable Souls
Phonse Jessome

978-177108-417-8

Lunenburg
Keith Baker

978-177108-309-6